Death in Earnest

A Mallard Melodrama
Book 2
R J Williams

For Felicity Butcher, my tutor,
who encouraged me
all those years ago.

Other books by R J Williams

A Fitting End

Sovereign Risk

Chapter 1

Mary Phillips was late, not egregiously so but enough to cause some inconvenience to Elsie, Verity's cook and housekeeper.

"I'll hold off on the spatchcock then. The soup's simmering so I'll not start on anything else until I hear from you," Elsie said, turning abruptly on her heel and returning to the kitchen.

Verity shrugged and turned an amused glance on her brother, Mortimer, sitting languidly by the parlour fire, swinging his pocket watch to and fro.

"Yes, Mortimer. There's no need for sarcasm. She'll be here soon."

"I dare say. What was it she called me last time?"

"A conceited, self-satisfied dilettante. I think that was it, and don't pretend to be offended, you're as fond of her as I."

Minutes later, a rapid series of taps on the front door signalled Mary's arrival. Verity rose and stepped into the hallway. "It's all right, Elsie, I'll answer it," she called out, not wishing to risk further displeasure from that quarter.

"Did something delay you?" she asked, helping Mary to take off her coat and hat.

"Oh Gosh. I am a bit late, aren't I? No excuses, I'm afraid. Just lost track of time."

"Never mind. Come on through."

Mary's lateness was hardly a surprise. Easily distracted and often lost in thought, punctuality was not her strong suit. She and Verity had first become acquainted two years earlier through a common love of music.

At the invitation of her great aunt Dorothy, Verity had attended a performance of Verdi's Requiem at the Royal Albert Hall and found herself seated next to a young woman whose friendly, outgoing demeanour had resulted in a friendship. Three years younger than Verity, Mary had secured a teaching position in a small private academy in Knightsbridge, catering for the daughters of the middle classes. But, as she was quick to point out, her passion lay in the theatre and a strong desire to make her way as an actress.

Mortimer rose as they entered the drawing room and extended his hand. With a brief handshake and words of welcome, he ushered Mary to a seat, receiving, as always, a warm smile of acknowledgement.

There'd been a time when Mortimer had wondered whether such an apparent sign of amity signalled an attraction on her part, but as they became more familiar with one another, it was obvious that she saw him as a rather amusing figure whom she enjoyed teasing as she would a brother.

Verity had, on occasion, played matchmaker by inviting one or other of Mortimer's wide circle of male friends and acquaintances to make up a foursome for dinner or a visit to the opera, but Mary had shown no inclination to form an attachment. So tonight, it would be just the three of them.

"Glass of sherry?

"Mmm – yes please, Mortie."

"Now, Mary, have you any plans for Christmas? I know it's still several weeks away, but Mortimer and I wondered if you would care to join us at Thorneycroft. It will be us three, plus Papa and our disreputable Uncle Ambrose; you'll like him, I'm sure," Verity glanced at Mortimer, whose look of surprise confirmed that this was the first time he'd heard of any such idea.

"Oh, that's very kind of you," Mary replied. "It's most unexpected. I'm quite taken aback. Oh, dear, that doesn't sound right. I mean, it's most thoughtful of you and, well, yes actually, yes, I'd love to."

"That's wonderful, isn't it Mortie?" Verity said, rising to press the bell, signalling to Elsie that dinner should be served.

"Uh – yes, yes, wonderful, capital idea," Mortimer ventured, knowing better than to question the matter.

Dinner passed without incident, the conversation consisting of light-hearted exchanges on their various day-to-day doings, and some discussion of current affairs. Mary joined in a little distractedly, waiting for the right moment to make her announcement. Elsie had just served baked lemon pudding for dessert when she spoke up.

"I've some news for you," she said in a strained, high-pitched voice.

Verity and Mortimer both stopped attacking their pudding and looked up quizzically.

"News, dear, what news?" Verity asked.

"Well… well, I've resigned."

"Whatever for, Mary? I thought Miss McGregor was very pleased with you. Did you hear that, Mortimer? She's resigned from McGregor's Academy."

"Of course, I heard it. I'm sitting right next to her, aren't I?"

"Let me explain," Mary continued. "It's nothing to do with my performance or anything like that. I've been quite happy there, though it's hardly an occupation that offers any real satisfaction. It's dull, Verity. Deadly dull. With every day that passes, I see my life slipping by. I…"

"Well, yes, you've said that before, but why this sudden decision? What will you do? Where will you go?"

"For heaven's sake, give the poor girl a chance to explain," Mortimer interceded. "Mary, you have the floor. Please enlighten us, and take your time," he added, glancing pointedly at his sister.

"It came out of the blue, really. But to get to the point, I'm going to be in a play, a proper play, I mean, not amateur dramatics this time. A professional company and a substantial part, if you please."

Mary's theatrical ambitions were well known to both Verity and Mortimer. A stalwart of one of London's better-known amateur dramatic societies, she'd played many parts over the years, gaining steadily in experience and reputation. Having developed several contacts in the profession, she'd started to press her case as an aspiring actress.

"It was Anthony Spencer himself who approached me. He's asked me to join his company for a forthcoming tour and guess what the play is to be."

Anthony Spencer was a name well-known to all three. One of the foremost impresarios in England, he was the driving force behind some of the most popular theatrical productions of the past decade. Mary had come to his notice the previous year, playing Raina in an amateur production of Shaw's new play Arms and the Man. He came backstage to congratulate her and they ran into one another from time to time at various theatrical soirees. Mary had suspected his interest in her to have another motive, but thus far, he'd behaved with the utmost decorum.

"My word, Anthony Spencer, eh?" Mortimer said, clearly impressed. "And the play?"

"Go on, hazard a guess."

"Oh, I don't know." Mortimer, whose theatrical tastes were more or less limited to popular operettas, struggled to bring anything to mind. "Wait a minute, I've got one - She Stoops to Conquer."

Mary and Verity snorted in unison.

"She Stoops to Conquer?" Mary gave him a pitying look. "What on earth made you come up with that? No, not even close."

"It's a contemporary work?" Verity interposed.

Mary nodded vigorously. "Oh, why don't I just come out with it – It's The Importance of Being Earnest."

Mortimer gave a low whistle.

"My dear, how marvellous," Verity said excitedly. "How wonderfully risqué, scandalous even."

"But wasn't the play closed down?" Mortimer asked.

The original production had been staged by the famous actor-manager, George Alexander, in February of that year at St James's Theatre, to general acclaim. However, the subsequent scandal arising from the Marquess of Queensbury's pursuit of its author, Oscar Wilde, through the courts and Wilde's imprisonment on a charge of gross indecency had mired the play in notoriety. After eighty-six performances, it closed.

"Yes, Mortimer, it was, but Anthony Spencer is convinced that the play should stand on its merits and is assembling a touring company to take it around the home counties and into the Midlands."

"When shall you start?" Verity asked.

"In January. We open in Windsor, and the tour will continue into the spring."

"What will you do in the meantime?"

"I have one month's notice to work out at McGregor's, then I'll be coming to you for Christmas. After that it's rehearsals and off we go. My goodness, I can hardly believe it's happening."

"And the part? What part are you playing?"

"Cecily – Cecily Cardew. I'm so thrilled."

Mortimer got to his feet. "May I propose a toast to you and a wonderful career on the stage? To Mary."

"To Mary," Verity echoed.

"Thank you both," Mary blushed at the attention. "Actually, I'm petrified. The thought of joining a professional cast is quite terrifying. I'll show myself up, I'm sure of it."

"Nonsense," Verity proclaimed. "You're obviously capable, or Anthony Spencer would never have approached you."

"Yes, I realise that, but I can't simply turn up to rehearsals cold. I must master my part first. Ideally, I'd like to rehearse the whole thing if I could find someone to read the play with me."

"Is that all? What could be simpler? We, Mortie and I, can read the play with you. I'll take the female parts and Mortimer can cover the male roles. Don't give me that strange look, Mortie. Of course, we must assist Mary. We have a month before Christmas, so there's no excuse. We shall find the time, and I'm sure that it will be great fun."

After Mary left in a cab, Verity and Mortimer sat silently near the fire while Elsie busied herself clearing the table.

"Goodnight, Elsie and thank you for a delightful dinner," said Verity as Elsie headed back to the kitchen.

"Goodnight, Miss Verity, Mister Mortimer," Elsie responded with the merest hint of a smile.

When the door closed behind her, Mortimer piped up. "What prompted you to invite Mary for Christmas? You might have told me first."

"Oh, I only just thought of it. It will be fun to have her along. She'll brighten the atmosphere. Remember how dull last Christmas was? Well, I intend to brighten things up this year. And she has only her sour brother and sister-in-law to go to otherwise."

"What on earth do you think she'll make of Papa, not to mention Uncle Ambrose?"

"She'll help to lift Papa's mood and as for Uncle Ambrose, who knows? I'm sure it will be most amusing one way or another."

"And rehearsing the play? You may have plenty of spare time to devote to it, but I have my work and all manner of other plans between now and Christmas."

"Mortimer, any plans of yours will have to accommodate the play. It's really not much to ask and we can't possibly let Mary down, can we?"

"Not now that you've promised that we'd help her, of course not. Oh well, all right, I'll do my bit. But I wish you'd consult me before charging in headlong."

"Good, that's settled."

Chapter 2

Thorneycroft Hall came into view as the carriage emerged from an avenue of elms. In the weak December sunlight, its honey-coloured stonework glowed dimly amid the curtains of ivy festooning the building. Standing in flat parkland, a mile or so from the village of Flaxminton, the house had its origins as a modest manor built by plain John Mallard nearly four centuries earlier. It had been extended and refashioned to suit the whims and ambitions of his descendants. While vestiges of the old house remained, the Hall, as it now stood, was largely the creation of the second baronet, built in the Palladian style. The formal, parterre gardens which once graced it had, in due course, given way to a supposedly natural landscape of smooth grassland, artfully positioned belts of trees and a serpentine lake, designed by a disciple of Lancelot 'Capability' Brown.

Verity and Mary sat side by side with a rug across their knees, their breath misting around them as they chattered. Verity called out points of interest as they proceeded at a quick trot towards the house. To their right, a glimpse of Frederick's Folly, named after the third baronet and, over on their left, the lake and grotto.

They'd travelled down from London by train as far as Bicester, where Higgins the coachman met them for the eight-mile journey to Flaxminton and Thorneycroft.

Mortimer preceded them by two days to attend to some estate business and it was he who now greeted them as they drew up at the steps below the main entrance.

"You're both very fortunate that the weather's set fair today, the last two days have been nothing but wind and rain," he said as the women alighted, then led the way up the steps and through the front doors into the vestibule where a maid took their cloaks.

Proceeding through the entrance hall, Mary looked about curiously. Her knowledge of country houses was confined to depictions in magazines and the descriptive powers of Jane Austen. While not the grandest of houses by any means, Thorneycroft possessed many of the adornments that Mary associated with such places. The walls in the hall and up the main staircase displayed portraits of past Mallards, interspersed with a still-life or two, and half a dozen alabaster busts in alcoves, the fruits of the third baronet's Grand Tour.

"How is Papa?" Verity asked Mortimer.

"He's having one of his better days. Played a little whist with Uncle Ambrose and Timmins this morning, quite lucid, actually. He's resting now. It remains to be seen whether he'll feel well enough to join us for dinner."

Mary had been forewarned that their father, the Reverend Sir Stanmore Mallard, Bt. did not enjoy the best of health. Suffering a delicate constitution since childhood, he was, at the age of fifty-eight, prone to a weak chest. His chief burden, however, lay in his increasingly severe bouts of depression, which had been a feature of his life since the tragic death of Lady Mallard five years earlier. Consequently, he'd withdrawn both from overseeing the running of his estate, which fell increasingly on Mortimer, and his duties as Rector at Flaxminton, which now devolved to his curate, Wilfred Timmins.

"Oh, Timmins. Not still about the place, is he?" Verity wrinkled her nose in distaste. To her, he represented the very image of Pride and Prejudice's odious clergyman, Mr Collins.

"No, he's gone off on the Lord's business, I'm happy to report," Mortimer replied. "Sadly, none of us will be able to avoid his presence over the Christmas period. Mary, don't let us sour your view of the man. However, we'd be glad to learn your opinion of the pompous ass."

Mary arched her eyebrows and decided it was best to say nothing in response.

"And Uncle Ambrose?" Verity said.

"They seek him here. They seek him there. Hasn't changed. Never know from one minute to another what he'll say or do. He's taken to rummaging around in the attic when he's not prowling around the estate. Generally turns up for dinner, though."

Uncle Ambrose was actually Sir Stanmore's cousin. Having spent many years on the subcontinent, he'd turned up at Thorneycroft Hall shortly after Lady Mallard's death with a hard-luck story about having been swindled of most of his life's savings by an unscrupulous business partner in Bombay. Offered temporary shelter by his cousin, he'd somehow contrived to remain under Sir Stanmore's roof. His eccentric manner and perpetual good humour provided a much-needed antidote to the Baronet's low spirits, so that he had, in a sense, become indispensable.

Verity led Mary up the marble staircase and along the gallery to an airy bedroom overlooking the lake and the deer park beyond.

"I thought the blue room would suit you, Mary. It has the best outlook. I'll have to leave you for the present and look in on Papa. He's becoming increasingly frail, I'm afraid.

"There's your luggage by the bed. I'll send Janet up to help you unpack. We dine at seven-thirty. I'll drop by at six-forty-five and take you down for drinks. If there's anything you need, just ask Janet. She's very obliging."

Chapter 3

Mary sat in the drawing room, enjoying the warmth of the fire, as Mortimer uncorked the champagne. Verity conveyed Sir Stanmore's apologies. He felt unable to join them for dinner, but hoped he would have the pleasure of making Miss Phillips's acquaintance the next day. "He's asked for a tray to be taken up. His appetite is much diminished," Verity explained.

As they lifted their glasses, a commotion outside had them turning their heads. The door swung open to reveal the lanky, ruddy-faced figure of a man in antique costume. Slashed doublet, ruffed collar, puffed Venetian breeches, stockings, hat and shoes of black velvet and a short vermilion cape worn jauntily over the left shoulder. Every inch the Elizabethan courtier, save for the ginger mutton-chop whiskers adorning his face.

"In God's name, Ambrose, what on earth are you playing at and what the devil was that racket?" Mortimer said, while Verity collapsed in a fit of giggles. Mary sat with her glass halfway to her lips, staring in amazement.

"Oh, never mind, just a bit of a contretemps with that suit of armour out there. I'll set it right later," Ambrose replied airily in a rich baritone, showing no sign of embarrassment.

"But your clothes, did you think we were having a fancy-dress party?" Mortimer persisted.

"Ah, aren't they simply wonderful? Found them in the attic. Couldn't resist putting 'em on. Have you been up there? It's a veritable treasure trove, old chap. All sorts of things… Oh, we have company, do we? Hello, my dear, and whom might you be?" Ambrose stepped up to Mary's chair, bowing with a flourish, and sweeping his hat off to reveal a large bald patch surrounded by a fringe of red hair.

Verity rushed forward to interpose herself between Mary, who sat frozen in her seat, and Ambrose, who had replaced his hat and stood looming over her, grinning broadly.

"Now, now Sir Walter, if that's who you think you are, give the poor girl some space," she said.

"Aye, aye your Majesty," Ambrose responded, skipping backwards and bowing again.

"Mary, this is Uncle Ambrose. Don't be fooled. He knows full well who you are, because Mortimer and I told him that you would be joining us for Christmas. I suppose every family has its eccentric side. This is ours."

"Pleased to meet you, Mr Mallard," Mary ventured, leaning sideways to peer at him around Verity.

"My dear young lady, the pleasure is all mine. What a great treat it is to have such a pretty young thing on the premises. Not married, are you? Can I hope? I feel an ode coming on. Shall I compare thee to a summer's day?"

"Ambrose enough!" Verity commanded. "We will go through to dinner and you will behave yourself. Mortimer, I will hold you responsible for keeping him under control."

Mortimer nodded gravely, stifling his laughter and offering his arm to Mary as Verity swept out towards the dining room.

Chapter 4

Mary woke at the sound of the curtains being drawn, admitting an encouraging shaft of sunlight.

Janet placed a tea tray on the dressing table. "It's a fine morning, miss. Miss Verity says she'll see you at breakfast at half-past eight and I'm to lay out your outdoor clothes for a walk around the estate."

So it was that two hours later, the two women were seated at the far side of the lake near a large willow.

"I hope you've now recovered from the shock of your encounter with Ambrose," said Verity.

"Well, yes, and he did behave himself at dinner; such interesting and amusing anecdotes. I found him most entertaining."

"Yes, he does have a talent in that direction. Just how much is true is another question, but there's no harm in him. The fact is, none of us knows much about his past life. He says he's never married, but who knows what really lies in his past? The main thing is that Papa values his friendship."

"He didn't appear at breakfast. Nor did Mortimer."

"Ambrose never appears at breakfast. As for Mortimer, he rose early to visit some of our tenant farmers with Clough, the estate manager."

"How is Sir Stanmore this morning?"

"Fatigued. He's decided to conserve his strength today. 'Verity,' he told me, 'I'm determined to enjoy Christmas Day with you and Mortimer tomorrow and, of course, I'll need my strength to attend church. I fear this may be my last Christmas on this earth and I want it to be a happy one.' I know in my heart he'll not see another," Verity whispered.

"Oh, I'm sorry."

"That's enough morbid talk. Come on, nothing like a good brisk walk to lift the spirits."

***

When they gathered in the drawing room that evening, Verity had regained her spirits. Being Christmas Eve, a group of children from the village entertained them with carols before being sent on their way with mince pies and small gifts. Ambrose made his presence felt, singing along lustily and regaling the children with quips and funny stories. To Mary's disappointment, he was dressed conventionally in a dark suit.

"We'll have a little entertainment when we retire here after dinner," Mortimer had forewarned her. "Verity plays the piano well and I don't mind admitting to a passable tenor. Some Schubert perhaps, and something from Gilbert and Sullivan. Would you be up to a duet, do you think?"

"Yes, of course, how delightful," Mary responded warmly, happy at the chance to perform. "Will we just be entertaining ourselves?"

"No, we shall have an audience. Papa will come down and Mr Timmins will call in for a mulled wine or two before he takes the midnight service at Holy Trinity, but most importantly, we'll have the servants, those that want to come along, that is. I should warn you, however, that Ambrose will insist on performing what he calls his party piece. I'll not spoil the surprise by telling you what it is. Just be sure you're not sitting close to him." Mortimer winked conspiratorially.

A jolly evening it turned out to be. Sir Stanmore came in leaning heavily on a stick and supported by his valet. He looked much older than his years, but despite his obvious infirmity, he greeted Mary in a strong, clear voice and spent a few minutes in conversation, showing a special interest in her forthcoming debut on the professional stage.

"Met Wilde once you know. Clever chap, I thought. Seems he was too clever for his own good in the end."

As she prepared to take her seat, she caught sight of a singular figure in the doorway talking to Verity. She knew instantly by his sombre clerical outfit that this must be Mr Timmins. Thin, tall and pale-faced with lank brown hair, his head bobbed up and down in a most distracting fashion as he spoke, transferring his weight constantly from one foot to another. Mary felt a strong urge to giggle at the sight of him and almost did so when Mortimer caught her eye and imitated the curate's actions. She dreaded an introduction, fearing that she would lose her composure but was saved from embarrassment when Verity abruptly led the curate to a seat, announcing that the entertainment was about to start.

The impromptu programme of music and song passed pleasantly. Mary and Mortimer performed some snippets from The Mikado, receiving particularly enthusiastic applause from the servants. As the music died away, it was replaced by subdued whispers. Mary looked around at the standing semicircle of maids and manservants, several of whom were grinning and nudging one another and nodding in the direction of Ambrose who had risen from his seat and turned to face his audience.

Ah, thought Mary, here comes the famous party piece.

The audience fell silent. Ambrose stood stock still, expressionless. Moments passed and Mary sensed anticipation building around her.

Then, in little more than a whisper, Ambrose spoke in a brittle, high-pitched voice. His eyes stared madly as he scanned his audience –

'Twas brillig and the slithy toves
Did Gyre and Gimble in the wabe;

The opening verse of Carroll's Jabberwocky held the room spellbound.

Ambrose's face contorted suddenly into a grotesque leer, teeth bared, arms raised above his head, fingers curled like talons –

Beware the Jabberwock my son!
The jaws that bite, the claws that catch!
Beware the Jubjub bird and shun
The frumious Bandersnatch!

Ambrose was a man possessed. He became the Jabberwock, the embodiment of hideous ferocity, arms flailing, head thrashing from side to side.

Then, in a flash, he became the monster's adversary, the 'beamish boy,' with his imaginary sword, all noble determination and courage in the face of the hideous Jabberwock

One, two! One, two! And through and through
The vorpal blade went snicker-snack!

His right arm swung once, twice, cleaving the fell beast, and Mary realised why Mortimer had advised her not to be seated too close. In his wild abandon, Ambrose's whirling arm took poor Mr Timmins on the temple, sending him sprawling onto the floor. Mary started from her seat to help, but Mortimer held her back, shaking his head, "Best to let him finish," he warned.

Ambrose didn't miss a beat. As Timmins struggled to rise, he planted his foot squarely on the curate's chest, as though he were the vanquished monster, "*O frabjous day! Callooh! Callay!*" he thundered, declaiming the final two verses and taking a triumphant bow. It was only then that he appeared to realise Timmins's plight.

Mortimer dashed forward to help the spluttering man to regain his seat and what little dignity he had left. The servants erupted in a gale of laughter and clapping, delighted at the spectacle until a sharp look from Verity subdued them.

"My dear Mr Timmins, do forgive me," Ambrose said. "When the Jabberwock's upon me, I fear I am not responsible for my actions. There now, let me get you another glass of mulled wine to revive you." He was quite unabashed.

"No, no," Timmins responded shakily. "Upon my word, sir, I am most put out. In front of the servants, sir? Shameful, shameful. No, I must leave for the church. What a to do.

"Sir Stanmore, Mr Mortimer, Miss Mortimer, I will take my leave. Good night."

With that, he shot a malevolent look at Ambrose and walked stiffly out into the hall. Mortimer followed and could be heard making soothing noises as he accompanied him to the door.

Mary looked across at Sir Stanmore, wondering whether the spectacle would have been too much for his delicate constitution, and was surprised to see him chuckling softly to himself. Waving to Ambrose, he said, "Your best yet, old chap. Capital entertainment."

Christmas morning, by contrast, was an anti-climax. A bitter wind blew from the east, driving intermittent showers. In the morning, Verity, Mortimer and Mary dutifully accompanied Sir Stanmore in the carriage to Holy Trinity. Ambrose had not appeared. It was well understood that he professed no religious beliefs, although he was given to speaking approvingly of Buddhism from time to time.

The service was taken by a seemingly recovered Timmins, and Sir Stanmore ascended the pulpit with Mortimer's assistance to read the lesson. His frailty was all the more evident as he gripped the lectern with parchment-white hands. Partway through, he paused and looked about vaguely. Verity was in the act of rising from her pew to go to his aid when he suddenly recovered his train of thought and continued, though haltingly, to complete the reading.

The carriage bore them back to Thorneycroft and the promise of a roaring fire and Christmas feasting. Mr Timmins joined their party but as no room remained inside the carriage, he sat up beside Higgins, shivering.

As yet, neither Verity nor Mortimer had effected an introduction between Mary and the curate. She wondered whether there was some reason for this apparent breach of etiquette, but concluded that neither of them considered

Timmins to be of any consequence. More a case of oversight than rudeness.

So, when they'd all gathered in the drawing room, she took it upon herself to acknowledge the man. Sir Stanmore had settled himself in one of two armchairs near the fire, the other being occupied by Ambrose. They sat heads together in conversation. Mary found herself standing near the window with Verity and Mortimer along with two ladies, neighbours of Sir Stanmore's. Miss Jemimah Aldridge and her sister Agnes, spinsters in their late forties, lived in nearby Dowling Court. Having no family of their own in the vicinity, Sir Stanmore had generously invited them to spend Christmas Day at Thorneycroft.

Mr Timmins was forgotten and stood awkwardly apart, appearing to be keenly interested in a watercolour in the far corner of the room.

Detaching herself, Mary went and stood beside him. He surely must have been aware of her presence, but he kept his eyes focused on the painting.

"Not a Constable, I fancy," she ventured.

Timmins turned to face her, removing the pince-nez through which he'd been examining the picture. "Ah, no indeed, miss, a quite different style of landscape, to be sure. A Scottish scene by Horatio McCulloch. A fine piece," he said, nodding repeatedly, in a most distracting fashion.

"Yes, isn't it? By the way, I'm Mary Phillips, in case you're wondering," said Mary, extending her hand.

Timmins stared blankly at it for a few moments, then held it limply. "Miss Phillips, yes, uh… pleased to meet you."

Mary retracted her hand, resisting an urge to wipe it on her skirt. The curate continued to stand there, staring disconcertingly. She felt at a loss as to how to proceed, but the reverberation of the dinner gong resolved the situation. Turning away, she hurriedly joined the others as they made their way to the dining room.

The Christmas feast was a revelation to Mary, who, since the death of her widowed mother, had been thrown on the mercy of her brother and sister-in-law at Christmas, both of whom had a parsimonious and pious attitude toward the celebration of Christ's birth. Far from an occasion of family joy, it was dreary and dispiriting.

Here, however, the atmosphere was wholeheartedly one of laughter and enjoyment. Ambrose had appointed himself master of the revels. As soon as Sir Stanmore had said grace, he placed his stamp on the proceedings, handing out an assortment of decorative hats; trophies, as he said, from the attic and other hidden corners of the house.

Two jockey caps, one in purple and gold and one in red and blue, were offered to the Aldridge sisters. A silver fireman's helmet for Mortimer. A dashing tricorn hat with gold trimming and a large green feather for Verity. Mary struggled to balance a tall, conical medieval headdress with a veil attached. Sir Stanmore adopted an imperial look with a chaplet of laurel leaves and Ambrose himself was magisterial in a black full-bottomed wig. 'My Judge Jeffries look' he called it. Which left only Mr Timmins sitting bareheaded at the end of the table.

"Ah, now then, Mr Timmins, what would suit you?" Ambrose said, as all eyes turned in the curate's direction. "Why, I have the very thing," he added, producing a large yellow pantomime turban and placing it unceremoniously on the man's head.

As they worked their way through the soup, ham, turbot, oysters, goose and rich plum pudding, Ambrose and Mortimer competed for attention with comic tales, anecdotes and witticisms. Verity joined in with her own brand of acerbic humour and even the Aldridge sisters were wont to contribute to the occasion, being particularly fond of Edward Lear's nonsense verse, most of which they appeared to have learned by heart. Mary, for her part, recounted some of her experiences in the theatre; one or two of which, she realised, were a little near the bone but were received with much amusement by all.

Not quite all. Seated to Mary's right, Wilfrid Timmins maintained a diffident silence. He'd been mortified by having the turban placed on his head, but dared not complain. Attempts by Mary and the Aldridges to engage him in conversation had proven fruitless. While a general air of bonhomie swirled around him, he withdrew further into his shell. However, what he lacked in social graces, he made up for in appetite, helping himself liberally to all the dishes and equally liberally to the champagne, hock and brandy.

At first, Mary imagined that one of Sir Stanmore's terriers had gained entrance to the dining room. She felt a momentary pressure on her right foot. It ceased, then she felt it again. This time it remained, moving under her skirt to make contact with her ankle. Lifting the edge of the tablecloth, she stifled a cry of alarm and disgust at the sight of the curate's boot pressing against her. Worse still, from the corner of her eye, she saw his flushed face turned towards her and smelt a sickening miasma of alcohol and halitosis.

Across the table, Verity rose to her feet. "Forgive me, Ambrose, I realise that you've yet not declared the feasting over but I feel the time has come to retire to the drawing room. Come, Mary, you and I will start the entertainment."

Stepping briskly around to Mary, she took her by the hand and extricated her.

"Thank goodness I saw what that vile creature was up to," Verity hissed as they entered the drawing room. As the others followed, Verity took Mortimer aside and whispered urgently in his ear. Timmins was the last to rise from the table and had just emerged from the dining room when he was gripped unceremoniously by the elbow and escorted smartly to the front door.

"Unfortunately, Mr Timmins has had to take his leave," Mortimer said breezily as he appeared in the drawing room some minutes later. "He sends his apologies. It seems the pressure of all his religious responsibilities has been a little too much for him."

Chapter 5

Verity and Mortimer were alone in the library. They'd returned from taking Mary to catch the train at Bicester, waving her goodbye with strict instructions to write as soon as she joined the touring company.

"It's been such a relief that Papa managed to enjoy Christmas," Verity remarked. "He told me that Mary's presence had been a real tonic to him."

"He said the same to me. Thank you for thinking of it."

"Even though you weren't very encouraging when I first broached it."

"Granted. I should have known better, I'm sure," Mortimer conceded ruefully.

"I fear that Papa's right, however, when he says that it will be his last Christmas. It's not only his physical decline, the spark of life is dying within him. We may as well face up to it and what it will mean for us. Or at least what it will mean for you as the heir."

"I've tried not to think of it. It always seemed a distant prospect in the past, something that would affect me in middle age, but suddenly it's staring me in the face."

"Well, at least you're acquainted with the condition of the estate."

"Yes, on the whole, it's in a satisfactory state, but I can see that some changes will need to be made. The world's moving on and we must move with it."

"Well, that's up to you, of course. The estate and the baronetcy will be yours. Primogeniture and all that."

"You needn't spell it out, Verity. I agree that it's unjust that everything devolves to the male, even though you're the firstborn. I dare say you'd make a better custodian of the estate than I."

"Hmm - well, never mind about that. I'm content to make my own way. You'll have to move down here from London and give up the law, too. Oh, and then there'll be another most pressing duty to perform," Verity added, giving Mortimer a meaningful look.

"Eh? Ah, yes, got your drift. Lord, I've not been planning to marry, but I suppose I'll have to think about it," Mortimer replied mournfully.

"Yes, you will. Some poor wretched woman will end up tethered to you."

Mortimer didn't answer. He got up, walked to the window, and gazed out over the lake.

"Penny for them?" said Verity.

"There's something else to consider as well. You know what I'm talking about," Mortimer replied, turning to face her.

"The skeleton in the closet, or should I say skeletons?"

"Yes, our skeleton, both figurative and real."

"It's a secret we'll have to live with, Mortimer. We both know that. We can never disclose it to anyone, even spouses."

"No. Although there's Benson, of course."

"Yes, of course, and he's as motivated to keep the Powell business a secret as we are."

***

The new year heralded great changes. Sir Stanmore died in late January. The news that his demise was imminent brought Verity and Mortimer rushing down from London. Ambrose met them at the door. For once, his irrepressible spirit was quenched. Silently he led them to their father's sickbed, where, at two-thirty on a bitterly cold winter morning, Sir Stanmore Mallard slipped peacefully away.

Mortimer shouldered the burden of his inheritance. The legal niceties were soon dealt with and his time was taken up with the management of the estate, which left him little opportunity to dwell on the profound change in his circumstances.

Verity inherited a modest sum of money and a house in Normandy, which had been part of her mother's dowry. She also took possession of her mother's jewellery, which had been bequeathed to her following Lady Mallard's death but which she'd left behind at Thorneycroft until now.

"You must continue to live at Montagu Square for as long as you wish," Mortimer insisted, "forever if you want."

"Don't be absurd, Mortie, it would hardly do for me to be shuffling about the place once you're married. I'll stay on for now while I consider what I should do with myself."

Chapter 6

Anthony Spencer's decision to stage The Importance of Being Earnest, despite the notoriety of its author, had, in most respects, been vindicated. The opening night in Windsor's Theatre Royal attracted a capacity audience as well as a small, strident group of offended citizens who stood outside bearing placards exhorting the patrons to shun the work of that 'unnatural creature' Wilde.

By the third night, they'd melted away save for two determined ladies who continued to fight the good fight. After a week in Windsor, the company proceeded through Berkshire, Buckinghamshire and Oxfordshire.

Mary soon became accustomed to the peripatetic life of the touring company. Having lived all her life in London, with just the occasional visit to Southend or Brighton, she enjoyed the novelty of the towns on their itinerary and the simple pleasure of journeying through the countryside.

Her initial nervousness during rehearsals and the daunting opening night had passed, and after four weeks on the road, she felt that she was very much the professional actress.

Which is not to say that everything was rosy.

As promised, she kept up a regular correspondence with Verity which consisted, in large part, of her observations of, and opinions on, her fellow members of the company.

There were nine of them in the cast. The two male leads. Playing John Worthington and his friend Algernon Moncrieff, were Edward Crawford, once much spoken about as an up-and-coming young talent on the London stage but now, at thirty-five, showing signs of having passed his peak, and Dalton Dixon, a rakish dandy in his mid-twenties.

Lady Bracknell could not have been more aptly cast. Gertrude Monserrat had been treading the boards for decades. Now in her fifties, she exuded an air of impatient disdain for everyone around her. Rumours abounded of her tumultuous and even scandalous past, both on and off the stage.

Gwendolen Fairfax, the object of John Worthington's affections in the play, was played by Cynthia Grant, sister of the celebrated society portraitist Kingsley Grant. Confident on stage, she nevertheless displayed a diffidence verging on shyness when off it, keeping herself to herself.

Ingrid Lloyd was Mary's favourite. A no-nonsense Liverpudlian, she played Miss Prism.

The remaining members, playing the minor roles of Canon Chasuble, Merriman and Lane, were three old stagers: Frederick Clarke, Sidney Fuller and Arthur Thomas. They all had a long history in the theatre but seemed to have been typecast as supporting players throughout their careers. Bachelors to a man, they formed a little clique of their own, centred on drinking and card-playing in their leisure hours.

In addition to the cast, there was Phillip Aspinall, the director; Adam Clews, the assistant stage manager; and Lizzie James, general dogsbody and dresser.

The following excerpts from Mary's letters to Verity contain some of her impressions of her fellow company members:

My dear, one discovers all sorts of interesting snippets about people the more one spends time in their company. You know how I wrote about Edward Crawford constantly dropping hints about being a great favourite with the ladies, but having been, as he puts it, 'unlucky in matters of the heart'. Well, what a fraud! The fact is that he shares certain - 'preferences', shall we say, with the author of our play. Yes, really. One doesn't expect stage-door Johnnies to be waiting on the male lead, but I've seen him leaving the theatre discreetly with such men on more than one occasion.

/ / /

Dalton Dixon, you know, the fellow playing Algernon Moncrieff, is having trouble separating our stage relationship from real life. I have had to remind him that although Cecily and Algernon are lovers in the play, he should not, for one instant, suppose that such a relationship can exist off the stage. I have found it necessary to reinforce this message with a sharp kick to his shins on a couple of occasions. He appears to have taken the hint as he has transferred his attentions to poor Lizzie, our dresser.

/ / /

I must say, I'd hoped that Cynthia Grant and I might have become friends, given that our characters are so closely associated in the play. She's such an enigma, Verity. She has beauty and a wonderful presence on stage, she could have been born for the part of Gwendolen. But as soon as the curtain comes down, what a transformation! She retires to her dressing room and keeps herself very much apart. It's as though she has two entirely separate personalities.

/ / /

I find I'm developing a thick skin as time goes by. I was under no illusion about the acting fraternity. You won't find a more self-absorbed lot: hungry for praise, full of self-regard and quick to exploit weakness in others. Oh dear, that does sound as if they're all terrible people, which is not the case, of course. It's really Gertrude Monserrat that's put me in such a state of mind. Oh, that woman! She has us all in a state of agitation, waiting for her next verbal barb. According to her, I'm - 'a silly young amateur with an inflated idea of her acting abilities. What Anthony sees in her, I can't imagine. Well, no, I can imagine, and it's not the way she delivers her lines.' - Really, she said that in front of the entire cast. Everyone hates and fears her in equal measure, even the director.

Mind you, she's said far worse to Cynthia. Perhaps that's why she's so aloof, Cynthia I mean.

/ / /

You asked whom I most liked among the cast. Well, I'm bound to say that there's only one person that I've really warmed to. Ingrid plays Miss Prism, Ingrid Lloyd that is. She's the only one that seems entirely herself. No airs and graces or condescension. She can be quite blunt but not in a hurtful way and she's always been kind to me, I must say.

/ / /

31

I call them the three chums. Frederick Clark, Sidney Fuller and Arthur Thomas. They're the ones that play minor roles. Oh dear, that sounds as though I look down on them. I don't mean to, it's just that they have the smallest parts in the play. They're all old stagers who've forgotten more about acting than I'm ever likely to learn. The thing is that they've formed a sort of club within the cast. I gather that they've all worked with one another over the years. They're each of them pleasant enough, but one can sense that they feel somehow apart from the rest of us.

/ / /

Now here's some news for you. You'll recall that I wrote in my last letter that Phillip Aspinall, our director, had commended me for the way I'd handled the situation when Cynthia Grant froze on stage in Act Three. I must say I surprised myself with my presence of mind and the audience was none the wiser. Anyway, he has asked me to have dinner with him and, before you ask, there will be another person present, young Lizzie James. I gather she's actually his niece. He's most presentable, by the way, about thirty-two or so. I must say I'm looking forward to it.

Oh, and another thing, there was the most frightful row yesterday. Gertrude, as good as accused Adam Clews, he's the assistant stage manager, of stealing from her dressing room. She had mislaid a little japanned musical box which she always likes to play before performances. It's a superstition of hers, apparently. It was so ridiculous. Adam vehemently denied that he'd taken it, but she'd have none of it. It took all of Phillip's diplomatic skills to calm the situation. And guess what? An hour later she appears, to say that the box had been returned. Not that she'd had a proper look for it and found it in her dressing room, which is surely what happened, but that it had been returned, implying that Adam must have done so. It's left a lot of bad feeling, I must say.

Chapter 7

The playhouse at Chipping Handley was a reminder of the town's more prosperous past. Once a thriving place, it had suffered from the expansion of the railways, which bypassed it in favour of Stokeford, ten miles to the west. The Empire Theatre belied its grand title. The small audiences it attracted meant that the circle was permanently closed, and the stalls were rarely more than half-full. The entertainment consisted largely of third-rate music hall acts and amateur productions by the Chipping Handley and District Dramatic Society. That it still stumbled along was due to the generosity of Sidney and Edgar Naismith, brothers and agricultural merchants, whose passion for all things theatrical found an outlet in their ownership of this fading relic.

The appearance of Chipping Handley on the tour itinerary had caused raised eyebrows and expressions of disbelief among the cast. Gertrude Monserrat had taken it as a personal affront.

"Anthony! This is surely an error. Chipping where? Never heard of the place. You cannot expect an actress of my stature to appear in some rural hamlet. It's unthinkable. I could have been at the Lyceum. Henry Irving is always asking me to appear. I'll not waste my talent on a gaggle of unwashed farm labourers and milkmaids. Outrageous!"

In his career as an impresario, Anthony Spencer had become accustomed to the inflated egos and hair-trigger emotions of performers. Not relishing a stand-up row in front of the whole company, he managed to draw Gertrude away to a quiet corner where, after several minutes of heated whispering, a truce was negotiated, involving the promise of a confidential fee as compensation for the injury to Gertrude's professional dignity that an appearance at Chipping Handley would represent.

Having smoothed the mother hen's ruffled feathers, he returned to the rest of the cast.

"Everyone, I appreciate that it may seem… incongruous, shall we say, that the Empire Theatre at Chipping Handley is part of our programme. It certainly doesn't measure up to the other venues at which you will be appearing. It's not some odd mistake on my part I can assure you, and I recognise that I owe you all an explanation.

"You see, it has a special place in my heart because it was there that I took my first steps in this wonderful business of entertainment. The town and the theatre were thriving then, though now, of course, those days are gone. Knowing that our tour would bring us into the area, I felt that I owed it to the town to acknowledge its role in launching my career by staging our play there. I apologise if it seems to represent a comedown for players of your calibre, but I would greatly appreciate your indulgence in allowing me to pay my respects to the place that gave me a start."

It was the sixth venue on the tour. Sandwiched between ten-day runs at Oxford and Cheltenham, Chipping Handley merited only four days on the tour calendar.

While the cast may have viewed the town with scorn, it welcomed them with open arms. Their opening night played to a full house. The Naismith brothers each gave a speech of welcome as did the mayor, and the curtain fell to thunderous applause and stamping of feet, which had Mary wondering how the fabric of the old theatre would cope. Even Gertrude Monserrat had the good grace to acknowledge the audience. Anthony Spencer, who had returned to London after the play's opening night in Windsor, had come down specially to renew old acquaintances and he gave a very personal speech of appreciation to the town for its part in launching his meteoric career.

When the second night had an equally rapturous reception, all the cast's misgivings vanished. As they gathered in the theatre the following afternoon, in readiness for their third night, their mood was buoyant.

Although they were now all thoroughly versed in their parts, Phillip Aspinall liked to put them through their paces. "Now then everyone, attention, please. Hearty congratulations on the last two performances. Now, I think, however, that we could sharpen up the beginning of Act Three. We'll take it from the top until the appearance of Lady Bracknell. So, Cynthia and Mary and Edward and Dalton, if you'd be so good?"

Mary dutifully stepped out onto the stage. Taking her position, she waited for Cynthia to deliver Gwendolen Fairfax's opening line. It didn't come. She'd assumed that Cynthia must have followed her, but there was no sign of her.

"Where's Cynthia? Didn't she follow me onto the stage?" she asked, looking at Edward and Dalton, who both shrugged.

"I thought we were all here," Phillip Aspinall looked around the auditorium. "Surely, she was here just now, wasn't she?" he added to no one in particular. "Did any of you see her?"

The cast looked quizzically at one another. "Now that you ask, Phillip," Ingrid piped up, "I just assumed she must be with us. I haven't actually seen her since last night's performance." Several of the others muttered that they hadn't set eyes on her either.

"Well, I can't say I'm surprised," Gertrude exclaimed. "The girl lacks discipline. I've had my suspicions for some time that she could not be relied upon, but did any of you believe me? No, of course, you didn't. Well, don't blame me if the play can't go ahead."

"Gertrude, please," Phillip pleaded. "Let's not jump to conclusions, least of all that the play won't go ahead. There's bound to be a simple explanation. Something must have held her up. Perhaps she's indisposed. Lizzie dear, would you pop across to the Bear to see if she's in her room?"

The cast awaited her return with varying degrees of interest. Gertrude stormed off to her dressing room. Edward and Dalton affected attitudes of bored detachment and sat smoking at opposite ends of the stalls. The three old stagers produced a pack of cards and sat at the side of the stage to play a few hands. Phillip, Mary and Ingrid stood together trying to make small talk while glancing nervously towards the back of the theatre for a sign of Lizzie's return.

"Ah, here they come now," Phillip announced.

Lizzie came walking swiftly down the right-hand aisle - but she was alone.

Phillip hurried up the aisle to meet her.

"She wasn't there," Lizzie said. "I knocked and knocked, but there was no answer."

"Perhaps she'd gone out. Did you ask the landlord if he'd seen her? She can't have just disappeared. She must be around the town somewhere. It's really too bad of her. She knew she was required here," Phillip grumbled.

"But that's just it," Lizzie said. "She has disappeared."

As they spoke, the cast members made their way up the aisle and gathered in a curious group at Phillip's shoulder. All save Gertrude, who had not emerged from her dressing room.

"Disappeared? What on earth do you mean, Lizzie? Disappeared? Impossible. For goodness' sake, girl, you're making no sense." Phillip's irritation threatened to turn into anger.

"For God's sake, man, stop browbeating her and let her speak," Dalton intervened, looking pointedly at Phillip. "Come on Lizzie, take your time and just tell us what you know."

"Yes, dear, just take a deep breath," Ingrid said, and pushed past Phillip to put an arm around Lizzie's shoulder.

"When I got no reply, I tried the handle of her door. It was unlocked. I opened it just an inch or two and called out, but there was still no reply, so I put my head around the door." Lizzie paused and took a breath. "When I said she'd disappeared, I wasn't being silly. Her bed was made and all her belongings had gone. There was nothing in the wardrobe or on the dressing table... and then I saw this on the pillow."

Phillip took the folded sheet of notepaper that Lizzie held out to him and gazed at it in silence. He remained hunched over it for several moments, then handed it to Edward before slumping heavily in one of the theatre seats with his head in his hands.

Edward read the words out loud as everyone looked expectantly in his direction

I AM SORRY.
IT'S BECOME TOO MUCH FOR ME.
PLEASE DO NOT SEEK ME OUT.
I NEED TO BE ALONE.
TRULY, I AM SORRY.

"That's all," Edward said. "Just that."

There was an awkward silence. Mary looked around, waiting for someone to react, but everyone seemed dumbstruck.

"What can she mean?" she ventured. "Does anyone know what she meant? What had become too much for her?" Her words seemed to break the spell. Everyone started talking at once in a confused babble.

She took the sheet from Edward. It was exactly as he'd read it. Five bare lines in neat black capital letters. Phillip appeared at her shoulder. "What the devil are we going to do now? We have two more performances here before we go on to Cheltenham. At least we have a few days there before we open. I'll have to tell Anthony; he's not leaving for London until tomorrow. God knows what he'll say," he said with a note of desperation.

"We've no understudy, have we?" Mary asked.

"Oh, well, there's Lizzie. She might carry it off if we give her a few days, but we can hardly substitute her for the entire tour. She simply lacks the stage presence for a part like this. Look, I must go and see Anthony right away," Phillip replied, then announced it to the cast, asking them to wait in the theatre until his return.

Mary watched as he walked dejectedly up the aisle. She still held Cynthia's note in her hand and thrust it into the pocket of her skirt, then detached herself from the others and set off after the director.

Anthony Spencer was staying at Sidney Naismith's house, a few minutes from the theatre. By the time Phillip and Mary arrived there, she'd explained her idea for saving the tour. She expected an immediate rebuff from Phillip, but felt there was nothing to lose. If the tour ended in an embarrassing failure, then her hopes of a theatrical career would sink with it. To her surprise, he listened.

Their interview with Anthony was fractious, to say the least, and all the more nerve-wracking on account of the presence of both Sidney and Edgar Naismith. They listened with dismay and incredulity as Phillip informed them of Cynthia's sudden and mysterious disappearance. Mary produced the note for Anthony's inspection. He read it without comment, shaking his head, then handed it back to her.

"Phillip, we've let the people of Chipping Handley down and you, Sidney and Edgar, who have given us such support, we have left you in an invidious position. I cannot begin to tell you how appalled and ashamed I am at this state of affairs. It's clear that our two remaining performances will have to be cancelled. If you would kindly excuse me, I will need to discuss this with Phillip outside."

In the street, Anthony turned to Phillip, eyes blazing. "I hold you responsible for this. Not only have you embarrassed me in front of the Naismiths and indeed the whole town, but I'm at a loss to know how we can continue with the tour. How the devil am I to find a replacement for the part of Gwendolen by the time we open in Cheltenham? Damn it man, we have just six days."

Mary felt close to tears. Phillip outlined her idea to Anthony but left it to her to explain it and attempt to convince him that it could work. In the end, he shrugged his shoulders, saying, "I will leave it to you, both of you. You will have this person, properly rehearsed, and ready for our opening in Cheltenham next week. You will inform me daily of your progress by telegram. If this fails the tour will be cancelled forthwith and I will ensure that neither of you works in theatre again. I'm returning to London. You, Phillip, will explain this to the cast."

Chapter 8

The next day, Verity read Mary's letter with a mixture of amusement and excitement. At first, the suggestion struck her as preposterous.

Could she spare the time? She had a couple of articles pending, but nothing urgent. In fact, this might present an opportunity. She could write an article, no, a series of articles, on the life of a touring actress in the modern theatre. Just the thing for *The Englishwoman's Review*.

Could she actually bring it off? She had read the part several times with Mary and Mortimer. She would need to refresh her memory, but already she could recall snatches of dialogue. Yes, that entrance halfway through Act One was quite fresh in her mind. She took her copy of the script from the bookcase and put herself to the test, closing her eyes when she got to Gwendolen's lines and speaking them from memory. Not bad. As long as she had a few days to rehearse, it could be done.

Learning the lines was one thing, but could she act? Could she take to the stage with a company of professional actors and hold her own? On this, she felt few qualms. When it came to confidence, she had enough for a whole company of actors. The prospect attracted her the more she thought about it.

Mary had written that the company was departing immediately for Cheltenham. If Verity agreed to join them, she should send a telegram addressed to Mary at the New Theatre and Opera House and follow on without delay.

***

"Ladies and gentlemen, it is my great pleasure to introduce to you Miss Verity Mallard who has agreed at short notice to take on the part of Gwendolen for the remainder of our tour," Phillip announced to the cast members gathered in the Green Room at The New Theatre.

"We have, as you know, just a few days before we open here in Cheltenham, a few days for us to put the unfortunate event in Chipping Handley behind us. Please make her welcome," he added, watching the faces of the cast and waiting for the inevitable backlash that would come from certain quarters when they learned that Verity was not only an amateur but a rank beginner.

It came as no surprise at all that Gertrude was the first to speak. "Miss Mallard, is it?" she intoned, fixing her gaze on Verity through a lorgnette, which she used on occasions when she particularly wished to emphasise her superiority as the premier artiste. Phillip blanched as Gertrude continued. Her voice and delivery were those of Lady Bracknell to a tee. Oscar Wilde might have written the part expressly for her. "Am I correct in assuming that you have no previous experience on the stage, that you are in fact not an actress but a contributor to certain journals or periodicals?"

Phillip was about to intercede on Verity's behalf but she held her hand up to stop him and turned to face Gertrude. "Miss Monserrat, is it? You are indeed correct in your assumption that I am a journalist and I'm proud to say that I am highly regarded in that profession. As to whether I am an actress? I can best answer that question by demonstration.

"Let me propose that we perform Act One, now, straight away. Not a rehearsal, a performance as though to a full auditorium. You all have the advantage of having performed the play together on several occasions, I have no such advantage. What do you say, Phillip?"

Gertrude interrupted before Phillip could respond. "Really, how ridiculous. I have no intention of taking to the stage at the behest of some amateur. Sheer impertinence."

Mary stepped forward, intending to express her strong support of Verity's proposition, but was forestalled.

"Well, I'm prepared to do it. Bravo to Miss Mallard, I say. If she's prepared to put herself to the test, then we must give her that opportunity," Edward Crawford said in his habitual, languid drawl. "What about you Dixon?"

"Capital idea. All for it," Dalton Dixon agreed.

Ingrid immediately signified her assent and the three old stagers nodded encouragingly. Mary clapped her hands in delight and beamed at Verity.

"I think that settles it," Phillip said. "Let's go through to the stage to take your places for Act One, from the entrance of Lady Bracknell and Miss Fairfax."

Mary and Ingrid watched from the auditorium as the play unfolded. Gertrude, being so clearly outvoted, had grudgingly gone along with it. Verity was superb, giving no hint of nervousness or hesitation, even when Gertrude deliberately attempted to throw her on a couple of occasions. Inside, her stomach was in turmoil, but she kept her head and concentrated. It was not just her spoken lines but her movement, demeanour and interactions with the other actors that would be judged under the intense scrutiny of Phillip and the cast.

At last, the ordeal was over. Verity felt drained and stood weakly at the side of the stage, hardly daring to look around her. No one spoke, but she could feel everyone's eyes turned in her direction.

A hand clap – once – twice - broke the silence. Then more hands came together, the sound swelling until the entire cast applauded with loud cries of bravo from Edward and Dalton. She looked up to see Mary both laughing and crying with joy and, to her astonishment, even Gertrude clapped, albeit half-heartedly, with her gloved hands. Her expression, however, was as sour as ever.

Phillip beamed. "Miss Mallard, Verity if I may, welcome to the cast of The Importance of Being Earnest. I shall have no hesitation in informing Anthony Spencer that the show will go on."

That night Verity and Mary sat in the small sitting room of the lodgings they shared.

"Well, now you can tell me the whole story. What have I let myself in for apart from two months of traipsing through the countryside with a gaggle of misfits, if your letters are anything to go by?" Verity said.

"Oh, not misfits. They do have their idiosyncrasies, but that makes the situation all the more interesting, doesn't it?

"So, this Cynthia Grant simply walks out of the play, leaving a note behind?"

"Yes, I've kept it. Wait a moment, I'll dig it out for you," Mary said. "It's in my bedroom." She returned and handed the note to Verity.

I AM SORRY.
IT'S BECOME TOO MUCH FOR ME.
PLEASE DO NOT SEEK ME OUT.
I NEED TO BE ALONE.
TRULY, I AM SORRY.

"Raises several questions and provides no answers," Verity commented. "Why is she sorry? Sorry for leaving you all in the lurch or sorry about something else? What is it that's become too much for her? You knew her. What do you make of it.?"

"Well, that's it. I can hardly claim to know her. She kept very much to herself. I can't say we ever had a conversation other than passing the time of day or perhaps discussing some aspect of the play."

"And the other cast members? What have they been saying about her? Surely, it must have been the chief topic of discussion when she left in so abrupt a fashion."

"Everyone seemed nonplussed, really. Gertrude made several scathing comments, but she was always critical of Cynthia. It's strange now that I think of it, but no one said a great deal about her at all. It's almost as though – no, that doesn't make sense."

"What doesn't make sense? You were about to say something. What was it?"

"Well, it's almost as though they were relieved. I can't say exactly why; it's just the feeling I had. Even Phillip - although he was in a mad panic at the thought of the tour having to be cancelled."

"Does anything strike you as odd about this message?" Verity handed the note back to Mary. "Not the meaning of the words, but the note itself."

"The note? No. Why? Do you see something odd about it?"

"Yes. Might it not be thought strange that it's not signed? Would you write a note of this nature and neglect to sign it? And there's another thing, it's written in capital letters. That's odd, surely? Apart from the fact that the note was discovered in Cynthia's room, there's nothing to indicate that it was written by her."

"You're right. It simply hadn't occurred to me. We should tell Phillip."

"Let's leave Phillip out of this for the time being. After all, it's only a theory. Let's change the subject. Actually, there is something I've been meaning to ask you regarding Phillip. Did you ever have dinner with him?"

"Oh, that," Mary replied. "Yes, I did. It was in Oxford. As I said in my letter, Lizzie also attended. It was pleasant enough, I suppose. He talked about himself. How he'd risen from a young supporting actor to become, as he put it, 'the most sought-after director in the contemporary theatre'."

"Typical male," Verity commented acidly. "And Lizzie, what did she have to say?"

"Could hardly get a word out of her. As the evening wore on, Phillip rather unsubtly suggested that she might want to retire to bed."

"Really. So, his motives were hardly innocent after all. Did he make any improper suggestions?"

"I never got to find out, Verity. Lizzie ignored him and stayed. Eventually, we parted and went our separate ways. All quite proper."

"Oh, were you disappointed?"

Mary shrugged. "Well, I was interested in learning whether he had designs. Which is not to say that I would have welcomed his attentions. Now let's get back to that note, shall we? What should we do about it?"

"Hmm… I think we need to know more about Cynthia Grant. Do you know anything about her at all? Where she came from? Her home?"

"I understand that she's related to Kingsley Grant. His sister, actually."

"Do you mean *the* Kingsley Grant?"

"Yes, the portraitist."

"Well, there's a starting point."

"A starting point? What do you mean? You're not suggesting that we should make inquiries about her. We're hardly in a position to play at detectives."

"No, Mary dear, of course we're not, but I know someone who can make inquiries on our behalf. An actual detective, in fact. I'll write to him."

Chapter 9

"Come in," Verity called, in answer to a tap on the dressing room door.

Lizzie appeared. "There's a gentleman to see you," she mumbled and promptly disappeared, to be replaced by a tall figure, resplendent in evening dress, cape and top hat.

"Mortie. What a wonderful surprise." Verity rushed to embrace him.

"Miss Verity Mallard, the new stage sensation. I simply had to come and see what all the fuss was about. I shall be in the front row for tonight's performance."

"How marvellous, but now I'll be all the more nervous. You should have let me know you were coming to Cheltenham."

"I'm actually on my way to Gloucester on estate business, so, naturally, I thought it would be a wonderful opportunity to see you and Mary en route. We'll have dinner together after the performance."

"Oh, Mary will be thrilled. This is our last night in Cheltenham. What a perfect way to end our run here. It's been very well received you know."

"Oh yes, I've read the reviews. And all this is because one of the cast left suddenly, I gather."

"That can be a topic for discussion at dinner. Now, don't think me rude, but I must get ready."

After the performance, Verity and Mary emerged from the theatre arm in arm with Mortimer, who escorted them to the dining room at the Queens Hotel.

"If tonight's performance is anything to go by, you can count this tour a triumph. I thought the curtain calls would go on all night." Mortimer raised his champagne glass in salute. "You, Mary, can be assured of a successful stage career and, as for you, Verity, could this be journalism's loss?"

"If you imagine that I'm about to change career, Mortie, then no, I have no such intention. Mary, as you correctly surmise, is well and truly on her way to great things, but I have other opportunities in mind where this tour is concerned."

"Such as?"

"Well, I've already promised *The Englishwoman's Review* a series of articles about an actress's life on tour. In fact, I posted my first contribution this morning. However, if I'm able to uncover the mystery of Cynthia Grant's disappearance, I'll have any number of editors keen to print it."

"Assuming that there really is a mystery. Her decision to leave may have a perfectly ordinary explanation. What do you think, Mary?"

"I agree with Verity that there's something strange about it. Here's the note she left behind," Mary said, withdrawing it from her reticule.

Mortimer scanned the note. "She sounds upset about something. Any idea what?"

"No, not specifically. She kept to herself. I hardly knew her. But there's the note itself, you see. Verity noticed it at once. It's not signed and isn't it rather odd that it's written in capitals?"

"Is it?" Mortimer handed the note back.

"Of course, it's odd, Mortimer. Surely, even you can see that," Verity said in exasperation. "It's distinctly odd and I intend to discover what's truly behind it, starting with finding out all I can about Cynthia."

"Really. You will continue with the tour, write your articles for *The Englishwoman's Review* and make enquiries about this woman simultaneously. I doubt that even your prodigious talents could accomplish all that," Mortimer replied, somewhat stung by her manner.

"Touché. Of course, I will need help. That's why I've commissioned George Benson to institute inquiries on my behalf."

"You've done what?

"Asked him to find out all he can about her."

"Has he agreed.?"

"Not yet. I only wrote to him this morning."

"And assuming that George has time to spare, how are you going to cover his fees?"

Verity smiled and reached across to squeeze Mortimer's hand.

Mortimer shrugged resignedly. "Very well, Verity. Oh, by the way, I came across an interesting story in the newspaper yesterday. It concerns Chipping Handley. Not a place one often hears about."

"Was it about the play?" Mary asked.

"No, it concerned a robbery. A Mr Sidney Naismith suffered the loss of several articles of value when his house was burgled. That's one of the owners of the theatre there. Did you meet him, Mary?"

"Certainly, Mortie. In fact, I visited his house and I must say that I was surprised at the valuable objects in his hallway and drawing room, which were the only parts of the house I saw."

"Really? What were they?"

"Paintings, a variety of delftware, some Georgian silver by the look of it. Oh, I'm no expert, but it certainly appeared to be a valuable collection."

"Hmm, what bad luck. One wonders how the thieves learnt of it."

Chapter 10

For George, it was a relief to step into the relatively fresh air of the street. Two hours spent observing a certain young bookkeeper, suspected of having stolen sums of money from his employer, had involved sitting in a dingy and claustrophobic drinking den. The fellow in question was well into his cups and had become a favourite among the seedy clientele, eager to take advantage of his hospitality. He was certainly spending freely. George left him to it.

It was late, but he called at his office to attend to his accounts before heading home. In the lobby, he stopped to unlock his postbox and withdraw the mail before trudging up to the third floor. Lounging in his chair, he began to open his correspondence.

He opened the fourth envelope mechanically and examined its contents. At the end of the first paragraph, he sat up abruptly.

After that fateful night when he and Mortimer had consigned Henry Powell to a watery grave, George had tried his best to put the matter out of his mind. He'd not felt any great pangs of conscience, but it was hard to dispel a certain dread at the possibility that their act of summary justice might be found out. At first, he'd dulled his mind with drink, but the demands of his business kept him in check and by Christmas, he'd resumed an even keel.

He'd heard nothing from Mortimer and was content to keep it that way for the time being. Then, in the new year, he'd received an invitation to attend a dinner at Mortimer's club, the Unicorn. It was then that Mortimer announced to a gathering of friends and close acquaintances his imminent departure for Flaxminton, succeeding his father to become the seventh Baronet.

"You must come and visit," Mortimer told him at the end of the evening. "I look forward to seeing you at Thorneycroft Hall soon and I'm sure that Verity would also love to see you again."

He'd heard nothing since, and wasn't sure that Mortimer had been sincere. Best, perhaps, if they went their separate ways.

Now this letter. Not from Mortimer, but Verity. A request for his assistance to investigate the disappearance of Cynthia Grant. The name meant nothing to him. He read on. His brief acquaintance with Verity had been enough to impress upon him her towering sense of self-assurance. To learn that she'd become an actress somehow seemed unremarkable. If she'd announced that she'd become Empress of Russia, he'd be inclined to believe it.

So, this Cynthia Grant, who'd been part of the cast of The Importance of Being Earnest, had disappeared from somewhere called Chipping Handley, leaving behind an enigmatic note. Verity had reproduced it. The only additional scrap of information he had to go on was that Cynthia was supposedly the sister of Kingsley Grant. George knew that name, all right. Kingsley Grant was the most celebrated portraitist of his time. The darling of society ladies and a figure of considerable notoriety. There was nothing to indicate why Verity felt she must commission such an investigation, only an artful plea for George's help and the assurance that Mortimer would cover his fee.

Intrigued but wary, George decided to go home and sleep on it and consider the matter in the light of day. But that was a vain hope. He tossed and turned for an hour, then rose and re-read the letter.

He had other work. Could he spend the time? Why would he become entangled with Verity again? Look where it had got him last time. It was all futile. He penned a brief letter of acceptance.

First, he'd need to find out more about Cynthia. Her brother was the obvious source of information. Discovering his address was simple enough, but when he called at the Bloomsbury residence later that day, it was only to be told by a supercilious young footman that the master was not at home. His attempts to inquire when Kingsley Grant might be available were met with a disdainful sneer and the door being closed firmly in his face. At least that was the footman's intention. George's boot forestalled that move and the ten-shilling note he held up produced the grudging statement that the master was currently in the south of France and was not expected to return for six weeks.

Undaunted, he stepped back onto the pavement and hailed a passing hansom. "Where to guvnor?"

"Drury Lane."

The cab pulled up opposite the Theatre Royal.

The prim young man occupying the reception counter at the offices of *The Stage*, the weekly newspaper specialising in all things theatrical, was guarded. "Back numbers, sir?"

"That's right, I would like to examine back numbers of your newspaper. You do keep back numbers?"

"We do. But it is customary for those seeking access to them to make their requests in writing."

"Very well. Do you have some notepaper to hand? I'll write my request now."

"But it would require proper consideration. You can't expect to simply walk in and be granted access on the spot," the man responded huffily.

George took a deep breath. He considered offering money but thought it most unlikely that the fellow was susceptible to inducements. More likely that he'd send George packing.

"Perhaps I can be of assistance, Mr …?"

George turned to face the speaker, a plain woman with a mass of dark curly hair, approaching middle age. Her tone was friendly enough.

"Er… Benson, madam, George Benson.

"And I am Mrs Charles L Carson, Mr Benson. My husband is the proprietor. What is your interest in our newspaper? Are you in the theatrical profession?"

George considered spinning a tale, but thought better of it. "I'm conducting inquiries on behalf of a client, Mrs Carson," he said, smiling in the hope of disarming her.

"Indeed, how intriguing? Are you some sort of detective?"

"Yes, I am, and I believe that your newspaper will be of assistance in the pursuit of my enquiries."

Mrs Carson spoke to the young man at the counter, "you may leave this with me, Thomas."

"Now, Mr Benson, if you would follow me, we will see how we may assist your enquiries."

He followed her along a corridor and up a flight of steps, arriving at a large office on the first floor whose walls were adorned with photographic portraits of actors and actresses, several of whom George recognised as stage celebrities.

Mrs Carson seated herself behind a wide mahogany desk, waving George to one of two chairs facing it. "Now, what is the nature of your investigation, Mr Benson?"

"It concerns the disappearance of an actress. Miss Cynthia Grant," George said, then gave a brief outline of the events at Chipping Handley. "The fact is, that Miss Grant is something of an enigma. I am seeking to discover something of her background in the hope that it might cast some light on her disappearance."

"I see, and you think that you might find such information by consulting back numbers of *The Stage*?"

"Yes, that is my intention."

Mrs Carson sat, considering what she'd been told.

"Well, you are welcome to do so, of course. However, I may be able to save you the trouble. Have you heard of *The Theatrical Ladies Guild*?"

George shook his head.

"It's a charity of which I am the founder. I take it that a man in your profession is no stranger to what some might term the less seemly side of society. To put it bluntly, The Guild exists to look after actresses who find themselves with child - out of wedlock. We provide support to these unfortunate women and make no judgement of them.

"I would not normally disclose private information about recipients of our charity but I'm concerned from what you tell me that some harm may have come to Miss

Grant and therefore, I can disclose that I know her and have been pleased to help her in the past."

"Oh, I had no idea," George said, uncomfortably.

"No, well, such matters are kept private for obvious reasons."

"I would be grateful for any information you feel able to divulge."

"I first became aware of her three years ago. She was beginning to make a name for herself in the theatre. Gradually, she progressed from small parts to leading roles and received good reviews. She reminded me of my younger self. My stage name was Kittie Claremont, but I gave up the theatre when I married. I was fortunate, but many of my sisters in the profession find themselves in distress and I, in my small way, try to alleviate that distress."

She hesitated, uncertain of what to say next.

"Eight months ago, she approached the Guild. I sat with her here in this office. I recall the look of panic in her eyes as she told me her tale, an all too familiar one. She had just discovered that she was expecting, you see, and she knew that as soon as it became known, she'd be cast aside from the profession. I did my best to calm and reassure her, but there was no glossing over the fact that her career would be over with the grim prospect of having to rely on charity to get by. I feared for her safety."

"You thought she might do something desperate, harm herself?

"Yes, and that is all too often the outcome in these cases. But it didn't come to that. She lost the unborn child shortly after our first meeting. She came to tell me and thank me for my help.

"That was the last time I saw her. Her career continued and prospered. Her role as Gwendolen Fairfax in The Importance of Being Earnest was a wonderful opportunity. But it seems that she has thrown it all away. A great shame."

"Did she identify the child's father?" George asked.

"No. I asked her, but she refused to name him."

"There was no chance of his marrying her then."

"One assumes not. She would not have come to me if that were the case."

"No, of course. Did she mention her family?"

"I asked her whether she might receive support from her family. Her parents had both died, she said, which left only her brother. He's…"

"Kingsley Grant. Yes, I tried to call on him. It seems he's abroad."

"Mm, I gather he spends much of each year in the south of France. Did you suppose he might have some knowledge of her?"

"If one were in trouble, one's closest relative would be an obvious source of help."

"She was estranged from him, Mr Benson. She told me as much. Incidentally, he's not her true brother. She was adopted."

"Really? What were the circumstances?"

"I'm not aware of the circumstances. But I gained the distinct impression that Cynthia disliked Kingsley. Perhaps that's not the word for it. Feared him might be more correct. I believe there was something in their past that accounted for it. I can't be more specific than that. In fact, there's not much more that I can tell you."

"Well, I'm grateful for the information you've provided, Mrs Carson. Would you have any inkling where she might have gone from what she told you?" George asked in the hope of finding any avenue of enquiry to follow. Otherwise, it was looking like a dead end.

"None, I'm afraid," she replied, rising and offering her hand. "I regret I can't offer you anything more, Mr Benson."

George shook her hand and made his way to the door. As he gripped the handle, one more thought struck him. "Would you happen to know how she came into the acting profession?"

"Oh yes, she was a protégée of Anthony Spencer, the impresario. I don't know how he found her, but her whole stage career has been under his guidance. They were close. He must have felt her departure more keenly than anyone."

Chapter 11

Verity finished reading George Benson's account of his inquiries. The tour had moved on to Worcester's Theatre Royal, where Verity and Mary sat in their dressing room before the matinee performance.

"George Benson's drawn a blank," Verity announced.

"Oh, that private detective of yours," Mary responded, gazing intently into the mirror as she applied her makeup. "Has he failed to find any trace of her?"

"Her brother is abroad, it seems. Have you heard of a woman called Mrs Charles L Carson?"

"No, should I?"

"Apparently, she's married to the proprietor of *The Stage*. She's given George some interesting information. It seems that Cynthia was pregnant but miscarried."

Mary stopped applying her makeup. "Goodness, when was that?"

"About eight months ago. Begs the obvious question, doesn't it?"

"The father? Did Mrs Carson say?"

"No, she didn't know."

"Lord, Verity - not one of the cast?" Mary blurted out, her voice rising in shock.

"Well, there's a thought," Verity replied. "I think we can safely eliminate the three old stagers, don't you, and

Edward Crawford is otherwise inclined. That leaves dear Dalton, who I'm sure would fit the bill, or our esteemed director, for that matter. But we're talking about more than eight months ago. The company wasn't formed then. And there's one more piece of information that I wasn't aware of. It seems that she owes her career to Anthony Spencer."

"Well, so do I, for that matter, Verity."

"Yes, I realise that, but from what George says, there was a particularly close attachment between them."

A loud rap on the door interrupted their train of thought.

"Curtain up in five minutes, ladies."

***

Mary cursed herself as she hurried back to the theatre. There being no matinee on Friday, Verity had suggested an afternoon of shopping followed by high tea. In the High Street, Mary discovered, to her embarrassment and annoyance, that she'd mislaid her purse when she reached into her handbag to pay for a pair of gloves. Despite her protestations, Verity had stepped in and proffered the required amount to the shop assistant.

As they emerged onto the street, Mary searched her memory. Only two possibilities occurred to her: either she'd left it at their lodgings or at the theatre. The theatre was closer.

"I'm sorry Verity, I must look for it. I'll meet you for tea later," she called over her shoulder as she rushed across the road, dodging nimbly between the traffic.

"Where on earth are you going?" Verity shouted after her.

"The theatre," she heard faintly, as Mary gained the opposite pavement and hurried away.

At the main entrance, on Angel Street, she found that the doors were firmly closed. She trotted briskly around to the stage door. It stood ajar. Inside, a stout, untidy woman wearing a long grey apron was busying herself with a mop and bucket in the corridor leading to the actors' dressing rooms. She stepped aside incuriously as Mary edged her way past with a shy smile and a whispered thank you.

She continued to the end of the passage and turned right. Another five paces brought her to the dressing room that she and Verity shared. Pushing the door open, she made straight for her dressing table. There was no sign of her purse on it or in either of the two drawers beneath. She glanced across at Verity's dressing table, but it was bare. Nothing for it, she thought, but to return to her lodgings and look there.

The movement behind her was so sudden that she only caught the briefest impression of a figure as it darted through the open door. Footsteps retreated down the passage, running hard. By the time she'd turned and reached the doorway, they were getting fainter. Whoever had been in the room would be at the stage door and outside in an instant. She was unnerved. The thought that an intruder had been so close frightened her. She returned to her dressing table and sat down to calm herself.

A voice behind her made her jump violently, but her shriek of alarm was cut short at the sight of Verity in the doorway. She was not alone. Her right hand was wrapped tightly around the wrist of a young, mousy-haired creature, hardly more than a girl. In her left hand was Mary's purse.

"Oh, dear Lord, Verity, you gave me such a fright," Mary panted. "And you Lizzie, where did you spring from?"

Lizzie James looked down at her feet, avoiding Mary's gaze.

"I'll tell you where she sprang from, Mary. From this very room," Verity said sharply, looking down at the girl's bowed head. "She almost bowled me over as I entered the Stage Door - with this in her hand if you please," she continued, brandishing the purse.

Mary took it from her and checked its contents. The ten-shilling note and assortment of loose change were still there, as was the silver locket containing a few strands of her late mother's hair. Nothing was missing.

Verity propelled Lizzie into the dressing room and closed the door. "You need to explain yourself, Miss James."

Lizzie looked up defiantly. Her eyes moved from Verity to Mary and then to the door. Verity planted herself squarely in front of it, folding her arms across her chest. "You have a choice. You can either explain yourself to us or to the police."

"Please, Lizzie," Mary said. "Tell us. I'm sure that there must be a reasonable explanation. I've always thought of you as a decent type. I know we haven't been close, but I would hardly have thought that you would do anything underhand. Are you in need? Is that it?"

Lizzie's eyes flashed. She laughed contemptuously. "Underhand, eh? Who are you to call me underhand? You and high and mighty Miss Mallard here? I found the purse lying on the floor and was taking it for safekeeping. Didn't want that charlady out there taking a fancy to it."

"But Lizzie, you ran out of this room. You saw me and fled. That's what happened, wasn't it? You must have been concealed behind that screen in the corner."

"I've told you what happened, and it's Miss James to you. Call the police if you like, it's my word against yours. You should be thanking me, not accusing me. And I'll say she assaulted me and all, dragging me along the passage," Lizzie retorted, nodding in Verity's direction.

Mary, lost for words, looked helplessly at Verity. Lizzie's counterattack was so unexpected. She had no doubt the girl meant what she said.

Verity moved away from the door and stood face-to-face with Lizzie. "Very well, Miss James, we won't involve the police, but you will apologise to Mary or we'll have no choice other than to involve your uncle. Phillip Aspinall can deal with the matter."

Lizzie's snort of derision made Verity blink. "Ha, Phillip. My dear uncle. That's a laugh and no mistake. If you think he's going to do anything, you're way off the mark." She looked from one to the other with an amused expression. "You really don't want to make an enemy of me, you know. Little Lizzie, the dresser, the dogsbody, knows things, she does. You try to make life difficult for me and you'll regret it," she spat, pushing past Verity and scampering down the passage, laughing.

That night, the performance finished at ten o'clock. Afterwards, Mary and Verity retired to their dressing room along with Ingrid Lloyd and Edward Crawford, who, it seemed, had no admirer waiting at the stage door that evening. They shared a bottle of champagne while Edward indulged in a pungent cheroot.

At ten-fifteen, Phillip Aspinall put his head around the door. "Wonderful performance, my dears - you too, Edward," he beamed. "Just escorting Lizzie back to her digs, then I'll be at the Coventry Arms should any of you wish to join me in a nightcap." As he spoke, Lizzie appeared at his side and took his arm as he walked on, turning her head to look defiantly at Mary and Verity.

"Capital idea," Edward called after them. "I'll see you there, Phillip."

Ingrid resumed an anecdote about her experiences on the stage in Dublin when Verity interrupted. "I'll have to love you and leave you, I'm afraid. I can feel a headache coming on." Before anyone could respond, she was on her feet. Mary made to follow her, but a sharp look made her resume her seat.

Chapter 12

Lizzie sat in her room, brooding. She felt anger all right, but not blind, unreasoning rage. No, if she wanted to be revenged for the humiliation she'd felt that afternoon, it would take a clear head - and she would be revenged.

That Mary creature was by the by, she'd keep, but Verity Mallard was a different matter. Everyone had a weak spot. Lizzie was good at finding weaknesses and she'd find Verity's. She moved to the dressing table and started to remove the pins and combs from her hair. She was only partway through the process when there was a light tap on the door. With half her hair hanging down to her shoulders, she felt a wave of irritation at the interruption. Another tap, slightly louder. It could only be that half-deaf old landlady, she thought.

"All right, I'm coming," she called out, hurriedly tucking loose strands of hair behind her ear. As soon as she'd opened the door and laid eyes on the veiled figure on the threshold, she found herself being propelled violently backwards, her windpipe gripped tightly by a gloved hand. The door was kicked shut, and she fell back across the bed with her assailant looming over her. The grip on her throat tightened. She couldn't breathe, much less cry out.

With a rustle of silk and taffeta, her attacker sat astride her, pinioning Lizzie's arms with her knees. Her face was covered by a black veil but Lizzie had no need to see the person's face. She knew that scent.

"Now then Lizzie," Verity whispered, her head inches away from Lizzie's face. "It's time you learnt some lessons in the realities of life. Lesson one is that no one, least of all a jumped-up little trollop like you, threatens me or any friend of mine. Lesson two - if you persist, I will make sure that you regret it for the rest of your miserable life. Do you understand me?"

Lizzie tried to struggle, to free an arm, but Verity pressed down harder with her body and kept a firm grip on Lizzie's throat. "If you struggle, I'll hurt you, really hurt you. So be still," she commanded. The hard edge of her voice and the realisation that Verity was much the stronger of the two made Lizzie desist. She was no stranger to violence, the casual violence of a hard upbringing, but this was a calculated, controlled assault. In her experience, well-bred young women such as Verity were soft creatures. Not mentally soft. Plenty of them possessed a cruel tongue. But they were not given to physical brutality.

She made a muffled choking sound. It was no pretence. She couldn't breathe; her eyes bulged with fear and desperation. The grip relaxed, just a fraction, just enough to allow some air into her lungs, but leaving Lizzie in no doubt that any rash move on her part would have immediate consequences.

"You said that you knew things, didn't you? Back there in our dressing room, 'Lizzie knows things', you said. I've been thinking about those words and thinking of how you, the dogsbody, as you put it, are always hovering in the background: backstage, in the dressing rooms, travelling with us, sometimes sharing the same lodgings. You have eyes and ears and you use them, don't you? Use them to gather information - a little scrap here, a little scrap there, looking for weaknesses, is that it?"

Lizzie shook her head from side to side. No, she mouthed.

"You will tell me," Verity insisted. With her free hand, she took hold of Lizzie's loose tresses, twisting them tightly around her fingers.

"You know, Lizzie, I had a governess when I was a little girl. French, she was. And she could be the sweetest of creatures. But, when I misbehaved, and I often misbehaved, she changed. She could inflict the most painful punishments, and in the most artful way. No one could see what she'd done to me, but oh, she knew how to hurt. Verity tightened her grip on Lizzie's hair and gave a sharp tug, not enough to pull it out but hard enough to bring tears to her eyes.

"But there are worse things. Much worse things that I could do to you. You see, I am a Baronet's daughter. Did you know that? No? It's true. And that means that I and my family have influence. We know people, powerful people: magistrates, judges, and members of the government, for example. Oh, and we know doctors, eminent men. Did you know that doctors have the power to commit people to lunatic asylums? Yes, Lizzie, such places are full of unfortunates who have been deemed of unsound mind. Young women who are delusional, for instance. And you are certainly delusional if you imagine for one moment that you can exert any power over me. But then again, perhaps that is too conventional a way of dealing with this problem. Too domestic. Here's a thought. Imagine you're walking along the street one dark evening.

Before you've had time to be scared by that sudden movement behind you, you're trussed up, rendered insensible. Imagine waking to find yourself in some stinking ship's hold en route to the bordellos of Morocco. White women are much in demand there, I gather, even someone as plain as you. Sounds too fanciful? Put me to the test and you'll discover just how fanciful it is."

Lizzie was no fool, but she felt that even if Verity was exaggerating, the balance of power was not in her favour. She could only come off second best, a long way second at that. She blinked twice in acquiescence and relaxed her muscles to indicate surrender.

"Now then, Lizzie, I can see that my words are having some effect. Where do you keep these weaknesses? In your head? Perhaps, but maybe you keep a record. I'll wager you do. Something you keep safe. Your insurance policy. Your power over others can't be just your word, can it?"

Verity studied Lizzie's expression while she talked to her. Her initial, wide-eyed shock had given way to a neutral expression, staring blankly at the ceiling, avoiding Verity's gaze. All save for the briefest sideways glance at the wardrobe when Verity used the words – insurance policy.

"I'm going to release you now. Don't do anything you may regret, just keep listening. I'm going to search this room and look through your belongings until I find whatever it is you're hiding. Don't bother trying to deny it. Just accept that your little game is over. I'll make it easy for you."

Verity stepped off the bed and held out a hand to Lizzie, pulling her gently to her feet and drawing her over to the wardrobe. The girl came along quietly.

"In here?" Verity asked, taking hold of the handle. Lizzie nodded. "In the portmanteau," she said, dully.

The small brown leather suitcase lay on the floor of the wardrobe next to two pairs of shoes. Verity knelt and picked it up, feeling its contents shift as she carried it across to the bed.

It was locked. "Key," she demanded, holding her hand out. Lizzie put her hands to the neck of her blouse and withdrew a chain necklace with two keys dangling from it. She unclasped it and dropped the keys into Verity's palm. "It's the smaller key," she volunteered.

A wooden box and a large white bulging envelope lay within. The box contained an assortment of cheap trinkets and keepsakes. Verity picked up the envelope and examined its contents. There was a sheaf of notes, most of which were neat and precise but others were written in a spidery, childish hand. There were observations, rumours, and overheard conversations. The various entries had initials associated with them. A quick glance was sufficient to see the initials GM and EC occurring more than once. Also, PA. She wondered how many others might be revealed on closer examination, but that would have to wait. And Verity was particularly intrigued to see the initials CG appearing once. There were also letters, some perfectly scandalous photographs, newspaper cuttings and a private journal. Verity stuffed the contents back into the envelope and looked up enquiringly. "You've been a very busy girl, Lizzie. Blackmailing the entire cast, were you?"

"Not all of them. Some."

"Cynthia? Was that why she disappeared?"

"Ha, Cynthia!"

"What do you mean by that?"

"It was Cynthia that put me up to it, wasn't it? I only did it because she made me."

"Cynthia? Why on earth would she?"

"She didn't say."

"Very well. How did she make you do these things? No, let me guess - she caught you stealing, and she threatened to tell if you didn't do as she said. Was that it?"

Lizzie nodded. "Didn't think she'd miss a few shillings. Caught me red-handed."

"Why did Cynthia disappear, Lizzie?"

"How should I know?"

"Oh, Lizzie. Don't take me for a fool. I saw her initials in your handwriting. She'd hardly be blackmailing herself, would she? Anyway, I already know about her pregnancy."

"How could you?"

"Never mind how, I know. Just remember that I know a great deal more than you can imagine. There's no point in trying to deceive me. You discovered it somehow and decided to hold that knowledge over Cynthia. You've certainly got some nerve, I'll grant you that. Do you know where she went?"

Lizzie shrugged.

"I asked you a question." Verity grasped Lizzie by the shoulders and shook her hard.

"No, I don't, honestly, I don't," Lizzie answered, shocked by the sudden reminder of Verity's propensity for violence.

"All right. Now I'll tell you what will happen next."

Chapter 13

The last day of the play's run in Worcester dawned bleakly. A river mist spilled over from the Severn, blanketing much of the town. By late morning, it had begun to disperse under the influence of a half-hearted sun.

Mary and Verity walked arm in arm towards the theatre in company with Phillip Aspinall. A matinee and evening performance were all that remained before they moved on to Kidderminster's Theatre Royal.

Unexpectedly, the front doors were wide open and a small crowd of people was gathered on the steps under the watchful gaze of two constables standing in the doorway.

"Wait here," Phillip said as he eased his way through the onlookers and engaged one of the police officers in conversation. Mary and Verity moved to the foot of the steps. They couldn't hear what was being said, but the mournful expression on the constable's face and Phillip's agitated gestures had them rushing up the steps to join him.

"What is it, Phillip?" Verity asked.

His face was haggard, drained of colour. His lips moved, but the words wouldn't come. He took a breath and tried again. "Lizzie… is dead. In there, they found her in there."

"Where? How? Phillip, what have they told you?"

"Just that. She's dead. In the theatre. Good God Verity, I can't take it in."

Verity turned to one of the policemen, the older of the two. "Exactly what has happened, constable? This man is the girl's - Miss James's uncle. You must tell us what you know," she demanded.

The man eyed her narrowly. "I've told this gentleman," he said, pronouncing each word slowly and deliberately as though to a child, "all that can be divulged at the moment, Miss. I'm sorry, but those are my instructions. "

"Is your superior inside the theatre? We can speak to him. Come along Phillip," Verity said, not waiting for an answer.

"Now, you hold your horses, miss, and you, sir. You can't go inside and that's flat. Now either go home or wait until Inspector Clegg is ready to speak to you. Step back, please," he said, extending his arms to shoo them away from the door.

Verity said nothing, taking Phillip's sleeve and guiding him to one side. Mary joined them and looked at the crowd, which had swelled as more people gathered, in the way that crowds have of attracting others to them. She noticed Dalton Dixon and Ingrid Lloyd approaching. Verity had seen them, too.

"Mary, go and head them off, would you? The last thing Phillip needs is more of the cast bothering him. He's too distracted to talk to them now. Just tell them what we've been told and keep them out of the way if you would. No doubt more cast members will be coming along soon."

"Oh, very well. I'll do my best." Mary retreated down the steps, waving to Dalton and Ingrid.

Verity turned back to Phillip and tried to offer some words of comfort and sympathy. He stood staring into the middle distance. His lips trembled.

She wondered how long they'd have to wait before the Inspector appeared. There was little point in trying to talk to Phillip. He'd withdrawn into himself. She looked at the growing crowd of onlookers. All sorts of people were represented: old gentlemen, young women with perambulators, shopkeepers in aprons, ladies who had interrupted their shopping to indulge their curiosity, and young men with seemingly nothing better to do. One of them attracted her particular attention. Dressed in a shabby brown suit with knickerbockers and a grey cap a few sizes too big for him, the youth had stationed himself close to two matrons deep in conversation. He edged closer, looking around casually, and deftly fished a purse out of the handbag belonging to the stouter of the two women.

"You there," Verity roared. "Stop thief!" she shouted, pointing at the lad, who looked up like a startled hare and took to his heels. "Get after him," she called to the two constables. "Come on, he's getting away."

The older constable gestured to his companion, who pushed his way through the crowd and began running after the thief who'd just disappeared around the nearest corner. The two ladies set up a commotion when they realised what had happened, prompting the remaining constable to leave his position in front of the door in answer to their cries of alarm.

Verity thought for a moment, then took Phillip by the arm and gently propelled him through the doorway. They crossed the foyer and stopped at the swing doors leading to the stalls. "Phillip. Listen to me Phillip," Verity hissed. "You must steel yourself. Whatever we find when we go inside, we must be resolute. Let me do the talking. Do you understand?" Phillip nodded mutely.

As they walked along the aisle, a grim tableau revealed itself. The theatre lights were up, illuminating the interior starkly. At the right side of the stage were two men, their backs turned to the auditorium. One kneeled while the other stood close by, looking down at a prone figure, which could only be Lizzie's lifeless body.

They reached the front row and stopped. Verity felt Phillip's arm trembling under her grasp and gathered herself to speak. The kneeling man was in the act of getting to his feet and turned his head in their direction. He whispered urgently to his companion, who turned abruptly and advanced to the edge of the stage. "Who let you in?" he barked. "This is a serious police matter. You have no business being here. Who are you?"

If he thought that his hectoring and hostile manner would cow these unwanted visitors, he was soon disabused. "On the contrary, Inspector Clegg; I take it that you are he. We most certainly do have business here. This gentleman is Mr Phillip Aspinall, the uncle of Miss Elizabeth James," she said, nodding towards the body. "And I am Verity Mallard, a member of the cast of our play. You will please tell us what has occurred here."

Clegg stood with hands on hips, looking down at them. A man of medium height, heavily whiskered, with thinning dark hair cut short. Verity caught his eye and stared back challengingly. "Very well, Miss Mallard," he said after a studied pause. "It's quite irregular, but if you and Mr Aspinall take a seat at the rear of the stalls, I will come down presently and tell you what I can. Doctor Henderson here has conducted an initial examination and was about to present his conclusions to me. You will find one of your colleagues over there," he added, pointing to the far corner of the stalls. Verity turned to see a seated figure hunched over with its head in its hands. "Come, Phillip," Verity urged, guiding him back along the aisle to where Edward Crawford was sitting.

Edward looked up as they shuffled along the row of seats. His face had none of the handsome confidence of the leading man. He looked shrunken in body and spirit, surveying them through watery eyes, shaking his head. "Phillip, it's s-simply too awful," he stammered. "How could such a thing have happened? Poor Lizzie, our little Lizzie. I can't believe it. I really can't."

Phillip slumped awkwardly into the adjacent seat. Edward looked expectantly at him, but there was no response.

"He's badly shocked," Verity said gently. "We'd best leave him alone for now. How on earth did you get in here, Edward? The police were guarding the door."

"I… I found her, Verity. I hadn't intended to come to the theatre until later, but I was walking past on the way to that sweet little tea shop along the road to meet an acquaintance of mine," he said with a nervous glance to the side. Verity had a fair idea of the nature of the acquaintanceship. "The front door was wide open, which seemed odd at that time of day. Anyway, the thought struck me that my rather fetching plum fedora would be a better match for my ensemble than the hat I had on. It was in my dressing room, you see. So, in I marched, through the auditorium. It was quite dark. I had to feel my way carefully down the aisle. As I neared the stage, I lit a match to get my bearings, and that's when I saw her. Thought it was a bundle of some sort or a piece of discarded scenery, at first. I went up to the stage to satisfy my curiosity and now I wish to God I'd not thought of that damned fedora and just walked on by."

"You found her?"

Edward nodded. "I rushed out into the street shouting for the police. Made quite a spectacle of myself. Someone ran off to the police station, and they were here in minutes."

"Has Inspector Clegg spoken to you, Edward?"

"Yes. I told him what I told you and I identified the… I identified Lizzie."

Inspector Clegg's report was short and to the point. "Our initial examination of the body suggests that the deceased young woman - Miss James - died as the result of a fall. Doctor Henderson is of the opinion that her demise occurred overnight sometime in the early hours," Clegg explained, unemotionally. "The cause and circumstances of her death will be subject to further investigation, and I must request that you and the entire company remain here in town for the time being."

As he spoke, two men appeared at the back of the stage carrying a stretcher on which they gently lifted the body and carefully covered it with a white sheet. Under Doctor Henderson's direction, they proceeded backstage to the stage door where an anonymous covered carriage awaited.

"The company are assembled in the foyer, sir." The constable that had spoken to Verity and Phillip stood at the top of the aisle. "Shall I bring them in, Inspector?"

"No man, of course not. This is an investigation scene. I'll speak to them out there," Clegg replied testily.

"Would you be so good as to follow the constable?" he said, addressing himself to Verity, Edward and Phillip. Verity stood up and ushered Phillip and Edward towards the exit, then stopped to look back at the stage. The scenery had been set up in readiness for the next performance - Scene 1 - taking place in the morning room of Algernon Moncrieff's London flat. The stage set depicted a luxurious and artistically decorated apartment and pieces of suitably fashionable furniture were distributed around it. The centrepiece was a table on which afternoon tea would be served in accordance with the playwright's stage directions.

With the exception of the china tea service itself, which was always brought out just before the performance, everything was in place for that afternoon's matinee. Except that it wasn't. Everything was not in place. The table, which was normally positioned precisely in the centre, had been shifted. It stood adjacent to the spot where the body had lain. Indeed, Verity had noticed Doctor Henderson and Inspector Clegg closely observing the surface of the table after they had finished examining the body. Phillip was a stickler for the correct positioning of scenery. Why would anyone move the table to one side?

"Miss Mallard." The Inspector's voice interrupted her thoughts. "Outside in the vestibule, if you please."

Chapter 14

The inspector's patience was severely tested.

The company occupied the foyer in an excitable mass, buzzing loudly, with several conversations going on at once. Mary ran over to Verity, imploring her to tell her what was happening. Gertrude was holding forth to Ingrid and Dalton, and the three old stagers talked among themselves. Adam Clews, the Assistant Stage Manager, made a beeline for Phillip but received no acknowledgement. The director looked vacantly around, with Edward standing forlornly at his elbow. There were now three constables and a sergeant in attendance, also talking animatedly.

"Your attention, please," Inspector Clegg announced - to no avail, as the hubbub continued unabated. "Quiet, if - you - please!" he bellowed.

When everyone's attention had been gained, he again stated the suspected cause of death and that the investigation would continue, during which time the company was requested to remain in Worcester. This provoked an immediate, loud protest from Gertrude, with others also muttering their dissatisfaction.

Clegg was having none of it. "I need hardly remind any of you," he said, glaring at Gertrude, "that a young woman has met with a sudden and, as yet, unexplained death. I will require statements from each one of you and, until I have completed my enquiries, you will stay here in Worcester. That is not a request. A few days should suffice. Obviously, today's performances will have to be cancelled."

The dreadful news of Lizzie's death brought Anthony Spencer down from London. The following week's performances in Kidderminster were hastily cancelled and the whole future of the tour hung in the balance.

Two days after the awful discovery, Verity found herself sitting with Anthony and Phillip in a private room at Anthony's hotel. She'd spent the intervening time helping Phillip to deal with the aftermath. Mary had leaned on her for comfort and support. Indeed, the whole company had, to some degree, come to regard her as a calm and steadying influence.

She was among the first to be interviewed by Inspector Clegg. No, she told him; she had no information which could cast any light on Lizzie's death. Did he, she asked, have any further information as to the cause? To her surprise, he was quite open about it. It appeared that Lizzie must have fallen from the gantry above the stage. The principal cause of death was thought to be a severe injury to her head, which appeared to have made contact with the edge of the table beneath. Why she should have climbed up there, he couldn't say, but her body smelled strongly of alcohol. The most likely conclusions were an accident or suicide - but no suicide note had materialised. Verity said she had no reason to suppose that Lizzie was suicidal and that concluded the interview.

"I'll communicate my findings to Mr Aspinall when my investigation's complete," Clegg told her. "Thank you for your statement. I expect this matter will be concluded swiftly." And that was that.

If only he knew, she thought.

***

After her confrontation with Lizzie, Verity took charge of the envelope and its contents.

"All right. Now I'll tell you what will happen next," she'd said. "You and I are going to find a way to return the money that you've extorted from your blackmail victims and we'll also return or destroy the embarrassing material you've collected. It will be a very delicate matter, but it has to be done, and I can't guarantee that the police will not become involved. All I will say is that I'll do my best to help you. You're an extremely foolish and misguided young woman, but I would not see you committed to prison for your stupidity, if it can be avoided."

The Inspector was thinking in terms of either an accident or suicide. But this was neither. Several people had a motive for murder and, as far as Verity was concerned, a provincial policeman with little imagination would not suffice to get to the bottom of it.

Anthony Spencer gave every appearance of being on edge. Another calamity had affected his cherished production. He must now decide whether to cut his losses or soldier on and had summoned Phillip to a meeting expressly to make a decision. It was Phillip who suggested that Verity should attend.

"I've asked you along, Miss Mallard, because Phillip here tells me that you're the most level-headed member of the company. We have reached a fork in the road. One path, perhaps the only sensible path, is to call it a day and

82

disband the company. The other is to continue despite everything. Kidderminster must be cancelled, of course.

"The police need to complete their investigation, but I have it on good authority that it will be expedited quickly." Anthony paused and looked at Phillip. "And we must allow ourselves time to grieve. Phillip, as Lizzie's closest relative, has elected that the funeral will be here in Worcester, as soon as the police are satisfied."

"What makes you so sure that the police investigation will be completed quickly?" Verity asked.

Anthony flashed a look at her as if he was annoyed by her question. "Well, Miss Mallard, I fail to see how they can come to any conclusion other than that this was an unfortunate accident. Misadventure. It seems that Lizzie was a rather headstrong young woman and was given to acts of rashness from time to time. Isn't that right, Phillip? Not being too harsh, am I?"

"Oh… she was young, Anthony. I don't know that I would say she was rash. Young people sometimes lack judgement, of course, but…"

"But, the fact remains, Phillip, that she got herself up on that gantry when she was clearly affected by alcohol. We will never know what she was thinking at the time, but in my book, that counts as an extremely rash act. I'm sorry to be blunt, Phillip, but there it is."

"Do I take it that you are inclined to allow the tour to continue, Mr Spencer?" Verity said.

Again, she received a sharp look in response. What on earth does he want with me if he's affronted whenever I speak?, she thought. And was on the verge of putting her thought into words when Anthony abruptly smiled and slapped his hand on the arm of his chair.

"I see you are determined to get to the point, Miss Mallard. I like that. And let's dispense with formality - Verity.

"If I were superstitious, I might well believe that the play is cursed. Cynthia Grant's disappearance and now this. Divine displeasure because of the sins of the play's author, perhaps. Well, I'm a businessman. Superstition has no place in my calculations. Cynthia's disappearance has actually worked to our advantage, thanks to you. The publicity, you see. The leading lady disappears and her place is taken by an amateur who proves to be a natural acting talent. It hasn't escaped the attention of the press. Attendances have been higher since you stepped in."

"You flatter me, I'm sure," Verity responded, not certain whether she should feel pleased or uncomfortable. "Lizzie's death would surely bring the wrong type of publicity, would it not, and might it not be thought callous to continue under such circumstances?"

Anthony paused, examining the fingernails of his right hand. "There's a school of thought which holds that all publicity is good publicity. Perhaps that's true. However, I would prefer that this business is put to bed as quickly and discreetly as possible. No disrespect, Phillip," he remarked, patting his director on the arm.

Phillip nodded glumly, looking down at his feet.

Anthony turned back to Verity. "I want the show to go on. Yes, of course, I want to make it a commercial success, but I'm also thinking of the company. Premature closure will leave them in the lurch when they've counted on the tour having its full run. I don't want to let them down."

He spoke with a hint of emotion, but Verity wondered how sincere he was. She hardly knew the impresario, but she did know something about him. The initials AS appeared in the papers she'd taken from Lizzie.

"Anthony. Why have you asked me here? You've already decided on a course of action. I fail to see how my presence here is of any value to you. I am simply a member of the cast."

"Ah… Verity, you do yourself a disservice. You're quite unlike the other cast members. You have a shrewd intellect and the confidence to display it. And you are not dependent on the stage as the others are. You are financially secure. If the play folds tomorrow, you can return to your comfortable townhouse and your journalism. In short, you are the person I'm depending on to be the mainstay of this tour for its duration. Phillip won't mind my saying that he is at a low ebb. I look to you to be his support and, in effect, the leader of the company."

"I can't imagine that Gertrude, for one, would be content with such an arrangement."

"You can handle Gertrude with ease, Verity. None of us is really taken in by her fits of outrage. Underneath the bluster, she's a mass of insecurities. I'll leave her in no doubt that any concerted effort on her part to undermine you or Phillip will have serious consequences for what remains of her stage career. So, Verity, it all comes down to you. If you accept my request, the tour continues. If not, it ends here." Anthony sat back and drew a cigar from inside his jacket. Verity watched him perform the ritual of sampling its aroma, cutting one end and applying a lighted match to the other. As the cigar glowed and pungent tendrils of smoke drifted through the air, he fixed his gaze on her.

Verity stood up and pushed back her chair. Halfway to the door, she called out over her shoulder, "you'll receive my answer tomorrow – Mr Spencer."

Chapter 15

The show went on.

As Anthony Spencer predicted, the police inquiry was soon over. The next day, she and Phillip received word that the police had concluded that Lizzie's death was a case of misadventure and no further investigation was necessary.

"Phillip, are you satisfied?" Verity asked him. "It's as though the police have no real interest in conducting a thorough investigation."

"I was rather surprised," Phillip answered wearily. "I said as much to Anthony."

"And what was his view?"

"Well, he said that he'd spoken to the Chief Constable personally on the matter and had been assured that the case was cut and dried. 'We must accept their decision, Phillip, and put this distressing business behind us,' he said to me."

"Did he indeed?" Verity was about to press Phillip further on the subject when she saw his face crumble. He sobbed quietly, covering his face with his hands. She moved to comfort him.

He stood quietly in her embrace until he'd regained his composure. "I don't know what to think. Verity, I barely have the strength to deal with Lizzie's funeral. Help me, would you?"

"Of course, I'll help Phillip. Whatever you need."

"I must do something about Lizzie's possessions. She had little enough, but I'd be grateful if you would help me to sort through her things. Everything will be as she left them at her lodgings."

"Of course. Did the police search her room as part of the investigation?"

"I believe they went there to look for any sign of a note, a… suicide note," Phillip replied haltingly.

At the lodging house, the old landlady ushered them up to the second floor. "A terrible business, sir," she said as they stood on the threshold of Lizzie's room. "Fair shook me up, it did. I've had to keep the room unlet, of course."

Phillip looked at her blankly.

"The room," she persisted. "Begging your pardon, sir, but it's still occupied in a manner of speaking. I'll need—"

"Quite so," Verity interrupted. "You will not be out of pocket. Now, if you would kindly leave us," she added insistently.

As the woman shuffled stiffly downstairs, Verity led Phillip into the room and closed the door.

There was not a great deal to do. While Phillip watched vacantly, she stood on tiptoe to lift Lizzie's battered old trunk down from the top of the wardrobe and placed it on the bed. "I'll gather her clothes up and put them in here," she explained. It was locked.

"Phillip, did the police give you anything from Lizzie's… I mean anything that she had about her person, jewellery, that sort of thing?"

"Uh, the police? No, not them. The undertaker asked me what I wanted to do with her two rings and the earrings she was wearing. I said they should be buried with her."

"Was that all? Did they mention a chain necklace she wore around her neck.? With two keys?"

"No. No, there was no chain. Why do you ask?"

"I need a key to open this trunk, Phillip. She had two, one for the trunk and another for a small portmanteau."

"Oh, did she? How do you know that, Verity?"

"Ah, I saw the chain once and remarked on it. She explained about the keys," Verity replied, hoping that Phillip's curiosity was satisfied.

"How strange that it's missing," she remarked as she opened the wardrobe. "Here's her portmanteau, but that will also be…" she broke off and knelt down. The portmanteau wasn't locked. The lid was up. It was empty. The trinket box, which it had contained, was next to it on the floor of the wardrobe.

Phillip looked over her shoulder. "Is something amiss, Verity?".

"Amiss? Not really. Perhaps she misplaced the key somewhere."

There was little in the way of furniture in the small bedroom. Verity quickly looked under the bed and asked Phillip to lift the mattress. She pulled the bedclothes back and moved the pillows. There was no sign of the keys. Another look inside the wardrobe. Not there. A small dressing table was the only other piece of furniture. Its drawers revealed no more than some items of Lizzie's toilette and her underwear. Finally, she took Lizzie's pitifully small collection of clothing out of the wardrobe and checked any pockets before placing them on the bed.

"Ah well, there's no necklace here. Never mind, Phillip. Mary and I will find something to put these clothes in. If you've no objection, I suggest we take them to a charitable institution. Would you like to take the trinket box?" Phillip nodded.

Lizzie was buried the next afternoon. The brief ceremony was attended by the entire company, but Anthony was absent. "Had to return to London, urgently," Phillip explained. As they turned and walked away from the grave, leaving Lizzie's mortal remains within the dismal confines of the municipal cemetery, a light drizzle added to the air of dejection.

With their Kidderminster dates cancelled, the company had a few days at liberty before the play was due to open at Coventry's Royal Opera House.

Verity took the opportunity to make a brief visit to Thorneycroft and Mary was only too glad to take up the invitation to accompany her. Two telegrams were dispatched. One to warn Mortimer of their imminent arrival and the second to summon George Benson.

Chapter 16

"Of course, you're always welcome Verity, and you too Mary," Mortimer said, escorting the two women into the drawing room at Thorneycroft, "but why the mysterious reference to 'urgent business to discuss' in your telegram? And you've invited George Benson. I thought he'd drawn a blank with that missing woman. Cynthia Grant, wasn't it?"

"Yes, but now we have not only a disappearance, but a murder."

Mortimer raised his eyebrows, waiting for an explanation. He had ample previous experience with Verity's propensity to make shocking statements. Mary was less sanguine. "Verity, are you saying Lizzie's death was murder? Good heavens, why did you not tell me this before?"

"Because I needed to be sure in my own mind, Mary. My suspicions have now grown to the point that I'm certain that Lizzie was killed and that several persons had both the opportunity and the motive."

"What persons do you mean? How can you be sure that she was murdered? The police say it was an accident and now you come out with this… this theory? I don't understand." Mary looked at Mortimer to see if he shared her incredulity.

"Mary has a point, Verity," he said calmly. "May I suggest that you explain your reasoning to us? Naturally, your claims, coming out of the blue as they do, are bound to raise questions."

Verity looked from one to the other. "If you'd both do me the courtesy of hearing me out without interruption, I shall, of course, explain the reasons for my assertions. Please keep any further questions to yourselves until I have finished. I've not brought you into my confidence without careful consideration. Do I make myself clear?"

Mary and Mortimer nodded.

"Very well. I said that several people had a motive for murdering Lizzie. That is because our innocent little put-upon Lizzie was a blackmailer." Verity noted with satisfaction the astonished looks that greeted her statement.

"Remember when you came across her in our dressing room, Mary? She said she knew things. I discovered that she was perfectly serious. You see, she was in possession of information, damaging information, about some of her fellow members of the company. And she was using it to extort money from them. I believe that someone among her victims killed her. Now you can ask me your questions."

Mary and Mortimer looked at one another. "After you, Mary," said Mortimer.

"Oh, very well – who on earth was she blackmailing?"

Verity smiled. "I'm afraid the answer to that question will have to wait until George arrives. Has he communicated with you, Mortimer?"

"Higgins is on his way to Bicester to meet him from the London train. We can expect him around five o'clock.

Now, my turn for a question, I think. How is it that this Lizzie, who by all accounts was a young woman of no great accomplishment or intellect, should take it into her head to become a blackmailer?"

"Ah, bravo Mortie, I admire your perspicacity. It seems unlikely, doesn't it? The answer is that she didn't initiate the business but was the instrument of another. I'll save you guessing - that person was Cynthia Grant."

"Cynthia?" Mary cried out.

"Yes, and the irony is that Lizzie ended up blackmailing her. The pregnancy that George discovered. It seems that Lizzie also had that knowledge."

"How, on earth …?

"That I can't tell you. I would have made Lizzie tell me, but she was killed. Perhaps Cynthia disappeared because she feared that her reputation would be damaged by the pregnancy becoming common knowledge, or there may be another reason."

"This is all most intriguing," Mortimer interjected, "but let's take a step back. You assert that Lizzie was murdered, yet the police investigation concluded that it was an accident. "

"Yes, according to the police, Lizzie fell from the backstage gantry and struck her head on the oak table below, which was one of the props for the play. They also pointed to the fact that she'd consumed a quantity of alcohol. The implication was that she had climbed up onto the gantry and fallen because she was inebriated. Mary, I appreciate that Cecily Cardew does not appear in Act 1, but you will nevertheless be familiar with the stage set at the commencement of the play."

"Uh, yes. Algernon's London flat."

"Indeed, and the centrepiece is a table, is it not?"

"That's right."

"And when I say centrepiece, I do so deliberately because the table is placed at the exact centre of the stage."

"Yes, it is."

"Yet when I was in the auditorium when the police were examining Lizzie's body, it and the table were off to the right of the stage, viewed from the stalls, that is. The table is always centre stage. It had been moved and placed adjacent to the body and one corner had been smeared with blood to make it appear that Lizzie's head had struck it."

"Good gracious."

"My theory, as you put it, Mary, is based on that observation. In my opinion, Lizzie was struck on the head before she fell. Perhaps she'd been plied with alcohol beforehand. She was then carried up onto the gantry and pushed off it. Then the table was moved and smeared with blood to make it appear that the gash to her head was caused by striking the edge of the table."

"Why did the police not reach a similar conclusion?" Mortimer asked.

"Ah, I see you still have your lawyer's way about you, brother. The police investigation, such as it was, was undertaken in haste. It was perfunctory at best and I believe that pressure was brought to bear on the investigating inspector to conclude it quickly."

"How so?"

"I can't be sure, but it's possible that Anthony Spencer has influence with the Chief Constable. Yes, Mary, did you have another question?"

"Did you hear that?" Mary said, turning in her seat.

"Hear what?"

"I can't hear it now; it was a noise. There it is again; did you hear it?"

The sound of a stifled sneeze was soon followed by another.

Mortimer rose swiftly and went to a mahogany bookcase standing against the wall behind Mary's chair. Placing his hand over a spot on its carved moulding, he swung the whole thing out on hinges. The space behind was revealed, as was its occupant.

"You might give this priest-hole a dusting once in a while, Mortimer. It's set off the old hay fever," Ambrose Mallard said, emerging into the drawing room. "My word, what do we have here? Verity, my dear, what a pleasure, and the delightful Miss Phillips as well. I am doubly blessed."

Mortimer shook his head. "How long have you been there, Ambrose?"

"Oh, quite long enough, I should say. How exciting. Blackmail and murder. What lives you actors lead," he said with obvious relish.

"Ambrose, the conversation you overheard was highly confidential. Surely even you appreciate that the matters we have been discussing are of a most sensitive nature," Verity said forcefully.

"Oh, sensitive, yes, I should say so. If I could unhear it, then, of course, I would, but now that it's in the old noggin, there's no getting rid of it. Now, I know I come across as a bit of an old duffer from time to time. Well – all right, most of the time. But I didn't spend all those years in India just being an amiable eccentric. I appreciate that you have a serious business on your hands and I would like you to consider me to be an ally. It may be that I can render a useful service at some point."

Verity and Mortimer looked despairingly at one another, shrugging their shoulders in unison. "Well, Ambrose," Mortimer said resignedly, "as you say, you can't unhear it. But I beseech you, keep this knowledge to yourself. Oh, and by the way, it's not a priest hole. It's a passageway that our grandfather had built, leading to the back stairs. I have no idea why. How on earth did you find your way in there?"

"Ah, that would be telling, old chap. I'll wager that there's not a square inch of this old place that I've yet to discover. I'll give you all a tour sometime if you like."

Chapter 17

The contents of Lizzie's envelope lay spread out on the library table. The sheaf of handwritten notes was divided into two. One written neatly in Cynthia Grant's small precise hand, the other in Lizzie's childish scrawl. There were also some newspaper cuttings and a small pile of photographic prints placed face down. And a small book bound in crimson leather.

Verity waited while her companions seated themselves. Mortimer fixed his gaze on the assembled objects. Mary looked nervously at Verity, while George Benson appeared quite unmoved, looking casually around the library. Verity had acquainted him with her theory concerning Lizzie's death after his arrival the previous day. To her surprise, he'd made no comment.

"Welcome to the next instalment of my revelations concerning Lizzie's death," Verity said. "Mortimer, I trust that there are no secret chambers to concern us here, from which Ambrose could emerge."

"None, Verity, and I've prevailed on him to undertake an errand to Flaxminton this morning, so we can speak freely."

"Very good. Now, here in front of us, we have the material that Cynthia and her accomplice, Lizzie, used to blackmail their victims. I've taken the opportunity to examine everything here, but I'd urge each of you to make your own assessment. In short, we have the two piles of handwritten notes, these refer to several members of the company and enable us to deduce who was being blackmailed and why. The newspaper cuttings also provide further evidence to support the assertions detailed in these notes. The photographs I have placed face down to spare your blushes, Mortimer and George. I'm sure Mary will regard them with perfect equanimity," Verity said with a mischievous grin.

"Then we have this," she continued, picking up the book. "This is a personal journal. Indeed, it is most personal, not at all the sort of thing that its owner would wish to be made public."

"Whose is it?" Mortimer asked.

"See for yourself." Verity handed him the journal.

As he flicked through the pages, Mary watched, barely containing her curiosity. George remained impassive.

Mortimer took his time, stopping occasionally to pay special attention to the text.

"Well, Mortie?" Verity prompted.

"Hmm, it's not signed," he teased, aware of Mary's rising agitation. "However, I think this must belong to…"

"Aaagh, Mortie, for pity's sake." Mary's exasperation had reached boiling point.

"It's Gertrude Monserrat, Mary," Verity interrupted. "The scurrilous comments she makes about prominent people in the theatre and elsewhere in public life would be enough to put her career in jeopardy, never mind the risk of being sued for defamation. Add to that the revelations regarding her private life and we have a veritable treasure trove of blackmail material."

"Oh, do pass it over."

"Later, Mary dear. You can read it to your heart's content later. But next, I think we should turn our attention to these photographs. They are… graphic. Here Mortimer, you first."

Mortimer reached across the table. Acutely aware of the three pairs of eyes studying his face as he scanned each of the photographs, he deliberately maintained a blank expression, until the fifth image had him spluttering involuntarily. Regaining his composure, he gamely shuffled through the remaining prints and replaced them face down on the table.

"I would strongly suggest that you don't look at them, Mary," he said.

"Oh come, you can hardly expect me to sit back demurely while the rest of you examine them. I'm not a delicate shrinking violet. You might be surprised by what I know of the world," she replied archly.

Mortimer shrugged. "Very well. Just take a look at the first one, then."

Mary laughed and picked them up. "Honestly, Mortie, all you're doing is whetting my curiosity," she said, placing them on her lap and turning them over. "Oh… Oh, I see," she stammered, hastily passing them to George, her cheeks burning. "Yes, one's enough - more than enough."

George shuffled through them matter-of-factly and placed them back on the table without comment.

"Are you quite recovered, Mary?" Verity said, "and you too, for that matter, Mortie. I did warn you that they were graphic. George, given your line of business, I would expect that you would be the least shocked by them. What do you make of them?"

"Leaving aside the human subjects of the photographs, one thing that strikes me is that they all appear to have been taken in the same place – the same room. It's richly furnished - the rugs, cushions, that upholstered divan and those… interesting frescoes. It has all the appearance of a bordello catering for gentlemen of a certain persuasion, shall we say?"

"Could they have been taken surreptitiously, do you suppose?" Mortimer asked.

"I'd say not, the subjects are captured in certain – uh – poses. In some cases, they are looking directly at the camera. I'd say that they were taken with the knowledge and consent of the subjects."

"My word. Had they no thought of what might happen if these photographs became public?"

"Perhaps their desire to have a memento of their activities overcame such qualms. No doubt, they felt that the photographs could be safely concealed."

"Apart from the surroundings, is there not another obvious feature which connects all these mementoes, as you call them, George?" Verity asked.

"Of course. There are several persons portrayed in this series of photographs. Some appear in more than one. But there's only one who is present in all of them. One whom we might consider the central subject of the whole collection."

"That's Edward Crawford," Verity proclaimed.

"That makes two people with a motive to murder Lizzie," Mary observed. "I can quite see Gertrude in that light, but Edward seems such a gentle soul."

"Gentle soul or not, if you were confronted with material as potentially damning as that, might you not do everything in your power to protect yourself?" Verity said. "Be that as it may, there are more than those two to consider. I have the advantage of having examined these handwritten notes and the newspaper cuttings. They reveal more blackmail victims."

"Please enlighten us then," said Mortimer.

"Of course. According to the material at hand, Dalton Dixon, not his real name, was cashiered from the army for seducing his commanding officer's daughter. Phillip Aspinall, Lizzie's own uncle, is a bigamist. Anthony Spencer himself is also mentioned, though here the notes are less specific, they simply say that he is not all he seems. Intriguing."

Verity sat back, observing the reactions to her revelations.

Mary gave an extended monologue expressing her lack of surprise regarding Dalton Dixon, that she had always felt there was something not quite right about Anthony Spencer, and sheer incredulity with respect to Phillip Aspinall.

Mortimer advised that such assertions should be treated with caution and that any evidence underlying them would require careful examination.

George took the handwritten notes and shuffled through them. After a few minutes, he put them back and turned to Verity. "This is all very interesting, but what is the purpose of this meeting? What exactly do you propose to do with this knowledge and why have you invited me here?"

"Thank you, George. I thought I could rely on you to get to the heart of the matter. We have a situation in which the police, either wilfully or negligently, have failed to recognise that a murder has been committed. I'm making it my business to find out who killed her; the same person, no doubt, who subsequently attempted to take Lizzie's blackmail evidence from her lodgings."

"You mean that you intend to do the police's work for them, is that it?"

"Not alone, George. I mean that we will seek to find out which of the people I have just mentioned killed Lizzie. Then justice can be served… "

"Spare me your views on justice. I've heard them before," George fumed. "You assume far too much, at least as far as I am concerned. In fact, you and I need to have a talk, just the two of us.

"Would you both mind allowing Verity and me to have a word in private," he said to Mary and Mortimer. "It will only take a few minutes."

Mary cast an anxious look at Verity. "Come, Mary," Mortimer whispered in her ear, "let's take a turn outside."

Left alone with Verity, George resumed. "This will not be another case like Henry Powell, Verity. I won't allow it. And what gives you the right to drag Mary Phillips into it, or even Mortimer, for that matter? For heaven's sake, why must you interfere? You say the police have come to the wrong conclusion, but what if they're right? It's their job. All you have is a theory based on a table being a few inches from where you expected it to be. You have no evidence and maybe that's because there isn't any," he said, glaring at her.

She met his gaze calmly while he said his piece, then rose and went across to a side table bearing a decanter and glasses. Silently, she poured two generous measures of Mortimer's favourite single malt, handing one to George and resuming her seat. Looking him in the eye, she took a taste of her whisky.

"You're quite right, of course. I have no solid evidence. And it was presumptuous, if not a little unwise, to involve Mary. I grant you that. You say that you will not allow this to be a repetition of the Powell case, by which I take it that you would not countenance our taking the law into our own hands.

"To that, I agree wholeheartedly. My only aim is to find the killer and leave it to the police and the courts thereafter. But George, you should be under no misapprehension that I will pursue Lizzie's killer. I know what I saw on that stage and these," she said, indicating the objects on the table, "prove that several people had a motive for murder. I cannot and will not leave this matter alone."

"You could provide the blackmail material to the police."

Verity laughed scornfully. "Oh, George, you're surely not serious. That would mean betraying a number of innocent people - innocent of murder, at least. I only want to catch the killer, not ruin the reputations of the others."

George nodded. "Yes, of course. Forget I said it. If you're determined to press on, so be it. I'll leave you to it and get the train back to London."

"Oh dear George, do I have to beg? It's very much not my style. Go if you must, but I would be most grateful… Oh, please, George, will you just do one thing for me? I'll take full responsibility for investigating the people on the tour: Dalton, Phillip, Gertrude, and Edward. But Anthony is in London. Can you at least keep an eye on him for me – please, George?"

An uncomfortable evening followed. At dinner, Mortimer attempted to divert the company with small talk about the estate and one or two of his more colourful tenant farmers. Ambrose contributed an anecdote about waking to find a python sharing his bed in Mysore. Everyone studiously avoided any mention of Lizzy and the issues arising from her death. George left for London early the next morning.

"I'm sorry to have brought you down here," Verity confided to Mary at breakfast. "On reflection, I wish that I'd not exposed you to all this. I'll not involve you any further. You have your career to consider. Far better that you keep your mind on the play."

Mary put her coffee cup down. "Do you think so little of me that you believe I can simply be fobbed off in that way? It's condescending of you. I'll not be patted on the head and told not to be concerned with such stuff. I am involved, whatever you might say. If you're right, and I'm now of the opinion that Lizzie *was* murdered, then who's to say that it will end there? I'll be constantly looking over my shoulder, wondering which of them is the killer. No, Verity. To echo Ambrose - I cannot unhear what has been said. So, where do we go from here?"

"To Coventry, Mary. The play starts on Monday. We'll leave this afternoon, and you and I will plan our next steps."

As the London-bound train left the platform at Bicester station, George gazed out of his compartment window through the wisps of smoke and steam and wondered how he'd allowed himself to become ensnared yet again by Verity Mallard.

Chapter 18

Coventry marked the halfway point of the tour. It would also be their longest booking, at two weeks. Most of the company was ensconced in the same comfortable establishment, catering especially for travelling thespians. Verity, Mary and Ingrid shared an apartment with a cosy sitting room of their own. Edward and Dalton occupied similar quarters. Gertrude rejected the prospect of sharing accommodation out of hand and insisted on a suite of her own. The three old stagers found more modest lodgings elsewhere, as did Adam Clews. Phillip, however, had announced that he would be staying with an old friend of his.

Monday's matinee was the first time the company had been together since Lizzie's funeral. The hiatus had set them back. There was a strained awkwardness among them. Cues were missed on a couple of occasions and Edward clumsily spilt a plate of cucumber sandwiches in Act 1. Fortunately, by the third act, the cast had recovered their poise, and the audience seemed to have forgiven or forgotten their missteps by curtain fall.

"How on earth are you going to discover Lizzie's killer?" Mary asked as she and Verity took tea in their sitting room between performances. "I've refrained from raising the topic until now, but really, what is it that you propose to do?"

"I've given it a great deal of thought, and I believe there's a way of drawing him or her out."

"Go on."

"Well, I propose to use the play itself."

"What on earth do you mean?"

"I mean to extemporise, ad-lib, improve even. To be clear, I intend to introduce some dialogue into the script. Text whose meaning will be apparent to each of Lizzie's blackmail victims. It will show that I know each one's secret. Then we'll see what happens."

"You surely can't be serious. Phillip would not allow it, and how would you persuade any of the cast to speak your lines? It's not practical, surely," Mary protested.

"Ah, but Phillip will not know. After all, he's one of the blackmail victims. Neither will any of the cast members. You see, it is we who will deliver the lines; our characters, that is. Cecily and Gwendolen."

"Oh, you wish me to be part of this, do you?"

"Yes, Mary. Dialogue of necessity involves more than one. The play is all dialogue."

"And what precisely is the object you wish to achieve.?"

"That the killer will believe that I am in possession of the blackmail material. Therefore, he or she will attempt something and in so doing will be unmasked."

"For heaven's sake. You mean to expose us to a murderer? It's insane."

"No, Mary dear, it's a calculated risk. Lizzie was taken by surprise. Whereas we will be on our guard. She was alone, whereas we can support one another. Also, put yourself in the mind of the killer. The police have declared that Lizzie's death was an accident. What will her killer's most pressing concern be? It will be to lay their hands on the blackmail material. Would they want to risk killing again, particularly as it would mean murdering two of us? The police could hardly put that down to misadventure."

"Where is Lizzie's envelope, by the way?"

"In safe keeping, at Thornycroft. So, what do you say, Mary? Are you with me?"

"Hmm. Have I any real choice? - You do realise that there's a flaw in your plan, don't you?"

"Which is?"

"Anthony Spencer. He's in London. He will not be present to hear your clever alterations to Mr Wilde's play. We have five blackmail victims: Gertrude, Edward, Dalton, Phillip, and Anthony."

"Granted. But Anthony wasn't in Worcester at the time of Lizzie's death. He may have had a motive for killing her, but not the opportunity. Indeed, the same could be said of Cynthia Grant, could it not? Mind you, even if he's not the murderer, I'm intrigued. Whatever it was that laid him open to blackmail, I intend to find out. Where Anthony is concerned, I'm relying on George Benson to discover the skeleton in his closet."

Verity annotated their copies of the script with the new dialogue and they rehearsed secretly until Verity declared herself satisfied. By the fifth night's performance, they were ready.

In Act 2, Cecily and Gwendolen meet and discover that they are both engaged. The scene is set in the garden of the Manor House at Moulton. The two women have the stage to themselves. The other actors watch from the wings, as does Phillip. Assistant Stage Manager, Adam Clewes, is in the prompter's chair, but since the slip-ups of the first Coventry performance, he's had no occasion to prompt.

Thus far, the dialogue had been delivered precisely in accordance with Wilde's script and stage directions.

Cecily: Dearest Gwendolen, there is no reason why I should make a secret of it to you. Our little county newspaper is sure to chronicle the fact next week. Mr Ernest Worthing and I are engaged to be married.

Gwendolen: My darling Cecily, I think there must be some slight error. Mr Ernest Worthing is engaged to me. The announcement will appear in the *Morning Post* on Saturday at the latest.

Cecily: I am afraid that you must be under some misconception. Ernest proposed to me exactly ten minutes ago. (*Shows diary.*)

Gwendolen (*examines diary through lorgnette carefully*): It is certainly very curious for he asked me to be his wife yesterday afternoon at 5.30. If you would care to verify the incident, pray do so. (*Produces diary of her own*). I never travel without my diary. One should always have something sensational to read in the train. **Although I must confess that when it comes to sensationalism, I come a poor second to my mama, Lady Bracknell. Her journal would shake society to its foundations were it ever to see the light of day. Of course, she does not know that I have perused it. It would mortify her. But I digress.** I am so sorry dear Cecily if it is any disappointment to you, but I am afraid I have the prior claim.

Verity glanced into the wings as she delivered her altered lines. Gertrude's astonishment confirmed that they'd hit their mark. She also saw the general confusion among the company at this unexpected departure from the script. Adam Clewes gestured wildly from the prompter's pit. Ignoring him, Mary and Verity continued with the scene, awaiting their next opportunity.

Shortly, Edward and Dalton, as Jack and Algernon, joined them on the stage.

Cecily: There is just one question I would like to be allowed to ask my guardian.

Gwendolen: An admirable idea! Mr Worthing, there is just one question I would like to be permitted to put to you. Where is your brother Ernest? We are both engaged to be married to your brother Ernest, so it is a matter of some importance to us to know where your brother Ernest is at present **for as things stand it might be thought that his intentions are bigamous. That would hardly do, I'm sure you agree**.

Edward subsided into a fit of coughing to cover his confusion at this unexpected addition to the text. Offstage, Verity could see Phillip stiffen at the mention of bigamy. A second mark had been hit. Meanwhile, Edward recovered his poise.

Jack: Gwendolen – Cecily – it is very painful for me to be forced to speak the truth. It is the first time in my life that I have ever been reduced to such a painful position and I am really quite inexperienced in doing anything of the kind. However, I will tell you quite frankly that I have no brother Ernest. I have no brother at all. I never had a brother in my life, and I certainly have not the smallest intention of ever having one in the future.

Cecily: No brother at all?

Jack: None!

Gwendolen: Had you never a brother of any kind?

Jack: Never. Not even of any kind.

Gwendolen: I am afraid it is quite clear, Cecily, that neither of us is engaged to be married to anyone.

Cecily: It is not a very pleasant position for a young girl suddenly to find herself in. Is it?

Gwendolen: Let us go into the house. They will hardly venture to come after us there.

Cecily: No. Men are so cowardly, aren't they?

Gwendolen: **It is as well that they are not soldiers. Such cravenness would see them drummed out of the army.**

Cecily: **Indeed, or cashiered for some act of moral turpitude, such is their duplicitous nature.**

The two women left the stage, to a nervous silence. Edward and Dalton looked helplessly at one another until Adam's insistent prompt spurred them into action.

Phillip could hardly contain himself. Pointing furiously towards their dressing room, he marched them away from the wings.

"What the devil are you two doing?" he demanded.

"Doing? Why Phillip, we are simply indulging in some improvisation," Verity replied casually.

Phillip stamped his foot in annoyance. "It didn't strike me as improvisation. Those lines were rehearsed."

"Very well, let's call it experimentation, to spice things up a little."

"Ha, the foremost playwright of the age has written a play of exquisite wit and brilliance and you feel the need to 'spice it up,' as you put it. I dread to think what Oscar Wilde would have to say."

"Well, he's hardly in a position to complain at present," Verity retorted.

Phillip eyed her disbelievingly. "Lady Bracknell's journal, moral turpitude – what on earth made you introduce those subjects?"

"Bigamy too," Verity added.

Phillip looked away. An awkward silence was mercifully broken by Adam's appearance at the dressing room door. "Act Three, in two minutes."

Mary and Verity rushed away, leaving Phillip slack-jawed, incredulous and uncomfortable.

The third act and its revelations regarding Jack's, that is to say, Ernest's, parentage proceeded without incident, although a distinct air of nervousness was evident as cast members regarded Verity and Mary warily each time they delivered their lines. The famous scene in which Lady Bracknell berates Miss Prism for mislaying a baby in her care, twenty-eight years earlier, elicits Prism's admission that she had absent-mindedly placed the baby in a handbag. Cue Jack …

Jack: But where did you deposit the handbag?
Miss Prism: Do not ask me, Mr Worthing.

Jack: Miss Prism, this is a matter of no small importance to me. I insist on knowing where you deposited the handbag that contained that infant.

Miss Prism: I left it in the cloakroom of one of the larger railway stations in London.

Jack: What railway station?

Miss Prism: Victoria. The Brighton Line.

Jack: I must retire to my room for a moment. Gwendolen, wait here for me.

Gwendolen: If you are not too long, I will wait for you all my life. **You need only furnish me with some photographs of your dear self that I may gaze on you in the meantime.**

At this point, the stage direction reads – Exit Jack in great excitement. Judging by the expression on Edward's face as he left the stage, excitement looked more like sheer terror.

If anyone in the audience was sufficiently acquainted with the script to detect Verity's alterations, they didn't show it, and the curtain descended to prolonged applause.

Afterwards, in their dressing room, Mary and Verity reflected on the evening.

"Is it safe to talk, do you suppose?" Mary asked. "I'm expecting Phillip to come bursting in at any moment to berate us again."

"I think we've given him other things to think about. It's telling, isn't it, that he and the other members of the cast simply dispersed quietly at the end? Even Gertrude."

"I saw the three old stagers muttering among themselves and, in fact, Ingrid did ask me what on earth had possessed us," Mary replied, "but it would appear that your plan had the desired effect. The blackmail victims know that you know their secrets. So, what next?"

"That remains to be seen."

Chapter 19

Alfie and Dick Cotton made an unlikely pair of siblings, having little resemblance to one another. The senior of the two by eight years, Alfie's spare frame and gaunt, swarthy features, gave the impression of malnourishment, although he was no slouch at table. Dick was a good head taller, with a thatch of straw blond hair and an athletic build. This disparity in appearance naturally gave rise to conjecture as to their parentage, but Betsy Cotton was adamant that her late husband's mixed heritage was playing out in their offspring. "Our Alfie's the image of my 'arold but 'is old gran was from one of them Viking lands. That's where Dickie gets 'is looks from." The truth was somewhat more prosaic.

George Benson sat opposite them in a corner of *The Lamb and Flag*. "Got another job for us, Mr Benson?" Alfie asked. "Ain't seen you around since that job before Christmas. Dick and I was wondering whatever 'appened with that bloke – wot's 'is name? Powell, that was it, 'enry Powell."

"Oh, yes. Henry Powell. I wish I could tell you. Not one of my most successful cases, I'm afraid. There was a mysterious fire in that lockup of his, the very night you came to me, Dick. He just disappeared."

"Good riddance too," Dick said. "He was a wrong un all right."

"Ah well. Can't win them all. Anyway, I've got another person I'd like you to keep tabs on. I'm a bit tied up with other work at the moment, so I'll be relying on you two to do the legwork. Here's the man," he added, producing a theatre programme from his jacket pocket. Headed Spencer's Theatrical Entertainments Presents - The Importance of Being Ernest, it included photographs of Anthony Spencer and Phillip Aspinall on the cover. "This one," he indicated with his forefinger, "and here's his address."

Anthony Spencer's pied-à-terre near Grosvenor Square was no secret. His flat was often mentioned in the society columns of the newspapers as the scene of well-attended soirées for celebrities of the theatre and other fashionable types.

***

The morning after Verity and Mary's surprise performance, a large bunch of roses was delivered to their lodgings, together with a note addressed to both of them. In it, Phillip implored them to desist from any further alterations to the script. Its tone was conciliatory, an appeal to their good natures.

"Well, well," Verity said, passing the note to Mary. "Phillip is indeed a worried man. By rights, he should have torn strips off us, but the poor man's practically begging us to behave."

"Yes, I see what you mean." Mary scanned the note. "We are going to do as he asks, aren't we? After all, we've made our point now."

"What point's that then?" Ingrid's broad Liverpudlian accent announced her presence as she emerged from her bedroom. "Nice bunch of flowers, that. Which one of you has a fancy man then?" she added, taking a seat in their shared sitting room.

"Good morning, Ingrid. They're from Phillip actually," Verity answered.

"Oh, are they? If I was Phillip, I'd be giving you both your marching orders and no mistake. Here you are, hardly been in the acting game for five minutes and you pull a stunt like that. Should be ashamed of yourselves. Try that nonsense again and I'll drag you both off the stage myself. Just see if I don't."

"I dare say you would, Ingrid," Verity responded coolly. "However, that won't be necessary. Our little experiment in impromptu theatre is over."

Ingrid glared at her and rose from her seat. "I don't know what game you think you're playing, Verity Mallard, and as for you," she continued, addressing herself to Mary, "just be careful you don't throw away your acting career before it's started."

The matinee passed off without incident although a palpable air of tension pervaded the stage, which became even more intense when those points in the play which had been subject to Verity's alterations were reached. Afterwards, the rest of the company went on their way in silence, studiously avoiding Verity and Mary. The tension was considerably reduced in the evening performance, but again Verity and Mary received a wide berth.

The play entered its second week at the Royal Opera House.

As usual, Verity entered her dressing room to prepare for that day's matinee. Mary had stopped at a shop along the way to make some everyday purchases. "I'll not be long Verity. I'll see you in the dressing room in a few minutes."

Verity had just changed into her costume for Act 1 when the dressing room door opened. "Did you get what you wanted, Mary?" she called out casually.

Receiving no reply, she turned around. Three pairs of eyes regarded her coldly. Standing shoulder to shoulder, Gertrude, Edward, and Dalton loomed over her.

"Shut the door, would you, Dalton?" Gertrude said, breaking the silence. He pushed it closed.

Verity stood and faced them. "Yes, what is it?"

Gertrude stepped forward, planting her parasol in front of her and drawing herself up to her full height. "Still congratulating yourself on your little diversion, are you? That ridiculous conceit of yours, altering the script. How dare you treat us in such a manner? What on earth were you thinking? We demand an apology and an explanation."

Gertrude's eyes blazed in theatrical high dudgeon. Verity looked at Gertrude's companions. Dalton stared back at her with a thin smile while Edward shuffled and looked away.

Turning her gaze back to Gertrude, she replied. "Surely you know what I was thinking. It was plain from your reactions. My alterations to the play were designed to provoke a reaction. You know what I'm driving at, don't you?"

"Perhaps. But why don't you spell it out for us?" It was Dalton who spoke. He perched himself on Verity's dressing table, produced a cigarette case from his jacket and lit one.

Verity resumed her seat and waved Gertrude and Edward towards a chaise longue against the back wall. Edward promptly sat while Gertrude stood her ground for a few moments, then abruptly joined him.

"Very well," Verity began, "each one of you was being blackmailed by Lizzie James. You, Gertrude, on account of the contents of your diary. In your case, Edward, there were photographs of you of an exotic nature, and then there were newspaper cuttings revealing the dishonourable actions of a certain lieutenant named Harry Chambers - your real name, Dalton."

Dalton, who appeared to have taken over from Gertrude as spokesperson, laughed. "Bravo, Verity, now let me guess. You think that Lizzie was killed by one of us because she had these items, do you?"

"Since you raise the subject, Dalton, then yes, I think that is a possibility. Being blackmailed is certainly a motive."

"But the police investigated and found that it was an unfortunate accident, did they not? Do you say they were wrong? Have you any evidence to the contrary or is it just supposition?"

Verity was uncertain how to respond. The last thing she'd expected was to be confronted by three of the blackmail victims together. She hesitated.

The dressing room door opened and Mary entered breezily. "Sorry to have taken so long, Verity, I…" Her voice trailed off as she saw the others.

Dalton beckoned her in. "Mary, how nice to see you. Do come in and join us. Verity is just entertaining us with some hare-brained theory of hers. Would you like to hear it? But, of course, you already know, don't you?" he sneered.

Her first thought was to turn on her heel, but that would leave Verity alone with them. Silently, she made her way to her dressing table and sat down.

Dalton rose and closed the door, then resumed his seat. "Well?" he said to Verity.

"I have good reason to doubt it was an accident. I do not intend to divulge that reason to you. The murderer will know, in any event."

Dalton turned to Gertrude and Edward. "Do you two have any idea what she means?" he asked.

"Of course not," Gertrude answered. Edward shook his head.

"No, because neither of you murdered Lizzie and neither did I. Now that we've established that, it's time for you two to explain yourselves," he said, looking pointedly at Mary and Verity.

Verity stared straight back at him, saying nothing.

"The silent treatment now, is it Verity? Mary, come on, you're one of us. Can't you see that this whole business will hurt your career?" Dalton cajoled.

"Leave Mary out of this, Dalton. You have no reason to browbeat her. I discovered Lizzie's cache of blackmail material and no, before you ask, she was not blackmailing me. I made it clear to her that the material must be returned to its owners together with any money she had extorted, but before that could occur, she was… she died."

"You discovered it, you say? Interesting choice of words," Dalton said, stubbing out his cigarette in a small porcelain saucer decorated in the Chinese style that Verity used as a temporary repository for her combs and hairpins.

Her glare of disapproval left him unmoved. "So, we can assume that you still have them?"

Verity nodded.

"Then, Verity dear, would you please be so kind as to give them to us," Dalton continued, reaching for his cigarette case.

"I'd rather you didn't smoke in here," Verity said.

Dalton opened the cigarette case and met Verity's gaze. A mocking smile crossed his face for a moment, followed by a sharp click as he shut the case and returned it to his jacket.

"Thank you, Dalton. As to the items - of course I shall return them, but as I am yet to be satisfied that any one of you was not responsible for Lizzie's death, I will hang on to them for the present. They are proof that you all had a motive. When I discover the guilty party, then I will provide the relevant blackmail material to the police as… what is the term… corroborating evidence? The remainder, I will return."

"You arrogant, interfering little bitch!" Gertrude jumped to her feet, her face contorted with rage. "Who the devil gave you the right to stand in judgement over us? How dare you accuse us of murder? There was no murder or, even if there was, who's to say that you were not the killer? We have only your word that Lizzie was not blackmailing you. I'll wager there's some tawdry secret in your past, Miss High and Mighty. We know nothing about you. You come here out of the blue - you could be an escaped lunatic for all we know." Gertrude's voice grew shriller as her tirade unfolded until she was practically screaming, spittle flying from her lips.

She stood trembling with rage. Edward took her by the shoulders, murmuring soothing words until she was persuaded to resume her seat. As her anger ebbed, she subsided into tears, burying her face in Edward's proffered handkerchief. Verity looked helplessly across at Mary. Her composure had deserted her. As someone so accustomed to being the master of events, she now found herself at a loss.

Edward found his voice. "There's no point in carrying on in this vein. There's something you need to understand, Verity. You see, we were not in thrall to poor Lizzie. Oh yes, after Cynthia's disappearance, she tried in her awkward, ham-fisted way to extort money from us. You do know that Cynthia was the original blackmailer, don't you?"

Verity nodded.

"Well, that's another story, but when she disappeared, Lizzie had the temerity to think that she could fill her shoes, so to speak. She came to me and threatened to sell the photographs to the gutter press. It worried me at first. When Cynthia left, I'd hoped that the whole business was finished with. I gave Lizzie some money, just five pounds, to begin with, knowing that she'd come back for more. But then I realised that it was just a bluff."

"How did you come to that conclusion?" Verity asked.

"Thanks to me." Dalton rose from the dressing table and walked across to stand next to Edward. "She was a silly young thing. I'd taken a bit of a shine to her, nothing serious, just walked out with her a couple of times. And then she tries her blackmail routine on me. I almost burst out laughing. Really, there was no way she would have gone through with it. I played her along a bit and the foolish girl let slip that I'm not the only one, names Gertrude and

Edward, doesn't she? Anyway, I told her not to be such an idiot and sent her away with a flea in her ear."

"And then he came to tell me what she'd said," Edward interjected. "I told Gertrude, and the three of us maintained a united front where Lizzie was concerned. So, you see Verity, the truth is that none of us had the motive to kill her."

"Nevertheless, she was murdered," Verity insisted.

"As you keep saying," Dalton's tone was now showing irritation. "Since it's not us, perhaps it's the bigamist. You know what I mean. One of your oh-so-clever script alterations mentioned bigamy. Neither Cynthia nor Lizzie tried that line with any of us. But you know who it is, don't you?"

Verity crossed the room to the door. Holding it ajar, she waited while Edward helped Gertrude to her feet and the three visitors left without another word.

Verity resumed her seat at the dressing table, silently arranging her hair.

"Well?" Mary said.

"Well, what?"

"For heaven's sake, Verity, what do you make of that?"

"I'm not sure. What do you make of it?"

"You heard them. They had no motive. Lizzie was no threat to them."

"And you believe them?"

"Well… yes, I suppose I do. Don't you?"

Verity put down her hairbrush and faced her friend.

"I have no reason whatsoever to believe them since you ask. Obviously, they want me to return the blackmail material, and that was the main purpose of their visit. The rest is simply their word. Perhaps what they say about

Lizzie is true, although when I tackled her, it took a great deal of persuasion to get her to cooperate. They made it seem that she was easily browbeaten.

"There's something else that occurs to me, Mary. The three of them acted in unison in coming here and the more I think about the way Lizzie was killed it seems most likely that more than one person was involved."

"More than one. Why do you suppose that to be the case?"

"Lizzie was of slight build but, nevertheless, it would have been difficult for one person to carry her up onto the gantry."

"Oh, I see. So, you suspect the three of them?"

"I'm simply saying that it's likely that at least two people were involved. Interestingly, Phillip was not with them and it seems that they don't know that he's also a blackmail victim."

Chapter 20

Alfie Cotton had perfected the art of blending into the background. In a drab brown suit with a matching scuffed bowler, he could pass for a member of any number of menial occupations: clerk, bookie's runner, cab driver, barman. The teeming London streets were full of men just like him. Today, he was keeping an eye on Anthony Spencer's office on Shaftesbury Avenue.

He'd learnt in the space of a few days that the impresario was a creature of habit, arriving at his office promptly at ten in the morning and sallying forth at noon to lunch at one or other of the hostelries in Soho and around Leicester Square, where he would be joined by theatre owners, theatrical agents and the like. So far, neither Alfie nor his brother Dick had observed anything out of the ordinary.

At 11.45, Alfie had taken up position outside the premises and was glancing idly at his newspaper when Anthony emerged. Rather than heading off on foot to one of his regular luncheon rendezvous, he stood at the edge of the pavement, raising his stick to hail a cab. Alfie folded the newspaper and stuffed it into his jacket pocket, ambling unobtrusively to station himself a couple of yards away. A hansom cab pulled up at the kerb and Alfie edged forward to catch the destination above the traffic noise.

"Great Eastern Hotel," Anthony called out as he settled into his seat.

Alfie kept pace with the cab on foot as it made its way through heavy traffic. He'd reached Holborn when the press of horse-drawn vehicles eased and he looked around for a cab for himself. Anxious not to fall too far behind his quarry, he threw himself in front of a cab whose driver appeared to be oblivious to his outstretched arm. Ignoring the grumbles of the cabbie, he climbed aboard and stated his destination. Anthony Spencer's hansom had blended into the throng of traffic by the time they set off, but Alfie arrived just in time to spy Anthony at the hotel's entrance. Not often given to exclamations of any sort, he couldn't stifle an oath when he saw the two characters that Spencer had with him.

Bert Figgis stood a head taller than Anthony. His menacing bulk was encased in a dark tweed coat that reached almost to his ankles. He sported a battered topper on his bald head and held a heavy stick with a dull, bulbous brass handle in his left hand. There was no mistaking that brutish face with its crooked pugilist's nose and the eyes of a dead halibut.

As though to compensate for Bert's intimidating stature, his youthful companion was a slight young gent. His tailored suit, gleaming boots and bowler tilted rakishly, gave him a dandyish, not to say effete, appearance. But Jackie O'Doyle's flamboyance belied his reputation for extreme violence.

The Bishopsgate Mob was rightly feared as one of the most notorious criminal gangs in London. From their heartland in and around Bishopsgate and Spitalfields, they thrived on extortion, robbery, illegal gambling, prostitution and any shady activity that made a quid. Violence or the threat of it was their modus operandi, including fighting for territorial dominance with other gangs. As their leader, Bert Figgis styled himself The Bishop, his principal lieutenants being O'Doyle, referred to as The Dean and, unusually, a woman - Ada Cole, The Archdeacon, whose fearsome reputation equalled that of the men.

Alfie hung back. He had no personal dealings with the two men but, as denizens of the East End, their paths crossed from time to time. He took a pair of clear glass spectacles from his pocket and pulled up his jacket collar as a simple disguise, following discreetly as Anthony and his associates entered the hotel. He watched them cross the foyer into the large, ornately decorated bar, where they sat at a corner table.

Alfie took up a position at the far side of the room, leaning against the bar counter, and ordered a pint of bitter. He watched from the corner of his eye as a waiter scurried across to Anthony's table to take his order, returning with a bottle of whisky and three glasses. Alfie was too far away to eavesdrop. It would be too risky to get closer and, in any case, the men were obviously at pains to keep their conversation private, sitting with heads close together, murmuring.

From time to time, one or other of them would glance around to make sure that no one was too close. Alfie could see that Figgis and O'Doyle were well known there, since the other patrons steered clear of their table. One unsuspecting pair of men made the mistake of approaching a neighbouring table only to beat a hasty retreat when O'Doyle directed a few words in their direction.

There was little to be gained from staying where he was, so Alfie finished his pint and left. It was almost an hour later, from his vantage point nearby, that he saw the three men emerge onto the street. Had they all left together, he would have followed in the hope of learning something about their business but, after a brief handshake, Figgis and O'Doyle walked away, leaving Anthony to hail a cab back to Shaftesbury Avenue. Alfie waited until Anthony's cab pulled away, then re-entered the Great Eastern Hotel.

"What the deuce would Anthony Spencer be doing consorting with the Bishopsgate Gang?" George Benson mused as Alfie sat in his office reporting on that day's events. "What do you know about them, Alfie? What use would a successful impresario have for a couple of east-end roughs?"

"Search me, guv. Whatever it is, it'll be dirty work of some sort."

"Pity you couldn't hear what they were saying."

"Couldn't get near enough. And I wasn't going to take any risks where those two are concerned. Bert might recognise me and I've seen what they can do to people, Mr Benson."

"Take your point, Alfie, but I can't leave it there. I'd like to keep Spencer under observation, but lord knows how long it might take to learn anything. We don't even know if he's going to meet them again."

"Ah, well that's where I can help," Alfie said brightly, taking a silver cigarette case from his jacket pocket. "I went back into the hotel after they'd gone and got hold of the waiter who'd served them. Spun him a tale about Spencer having dropped this on the pavement outside. Acted the innocent and asked if he'd seen a gent with two other men in the bar and did he know how I might find the gent to give him the cigarette case? 'Would he be a guest here?' I asked him. 'Oh, I don't believe so, sir' he says, all polite like, 'but if you want to find him, I did hear him say to his two companions as they were leaving that he'd meet them at St Peter's Street tomorrow at seven o'clock.' 'Oh, thanks,' says I, 'did he say what number in St Peter's Street?' He had to think about that. 'Oh, what was it now? Twenty-something? Or was it thirty-something? No, I'm not sure, I'm afraid.' So that's it, either it's twenty-something or thirty-something. Best he could do."

"Well, it will have to be enough," George replied. "St Peter's Street? Now then, that's in Islington. Had a client who lived near there, Devonia Road. Seven o'clock in the morning doesn't sound like Anthony Spencer's style, so tomorrow evening it is. As to the exact address, I'll just have to keep my eyes peeled."

"You sure about this, Mr Benson? The Bishopsgate Mob ain't to be messed with."

George nodded and pushed his chair back to open one of his desk drawers. "This will help if I run into any trouble," he said, holding up a short-barrelled pocket revolver. "The good old Webley British Bull Dog. It saved my hide more than once in my Pinkerton days."

Chapter 21

St Peter's Street extended all the way from Islington Green to Regent's Canal. The church near the junction with Devonia Road gave George a good view of the houses numbered in the twenties and thirties. He stationed himself in the shadow of the church door at six forty-five, wearing the same old reefer jacket he'd had on the night he and Mortimer had consigned Henry Powell to the Thames. A dark woollen cap was pulled well down over his ears. The dusk was chilly with a fine drizzle in the air.

The street wasn't busy. An occasional cab or horse-drawn cart passed. Such pedestrians as there were, walked by hurriedly, intent on reaching the warm comforts of home. No one looked in his direction. He scanned the street from left to right and scrutinised each approaching cab for signs of Anthony Spencer or the Bishopsgate men. At four minutes past seven, a cab pulled up opposite his vantage point. George pressed himself further back into the shadow of the church doorway and pulled his muffler up to his nose. The nearest streetlight was some distance away, but any doubts that the figure stepping down from the cab was Spencer were dispelled by his theatrical thank-you to the cabbie.

The address stood on the corner of St Peter's Street and a side road. An unremarkable end-of-terrace house with a basement. Spencer's knock on the front door was answered promptly, and he stepped inside. George couldn't see who'd admitted him. The door shut, and he resumed his watch, waiting for Figgis and O'Doyle.

Ten minutes became twenty. It was almost half past seven when George decided that they must already be in the house. The street was deserted as he crossed the road and stood at the front railings. No lights showed, either in the basement or any of the upper floors. The occupants must be gathered in one of the back rooms.

George had no plan of action in mind when he'd set out. Now he considered what to do. He'd learn nothing by continuing to watch the house from the street. On the other hand, it would be very risky to attempt to make an entry.

It was fully dark now. There was no sign of the moon through the clouds. With a quick look around, he took the few steps to the front door and stood on the threshold, listening. A gentle twist of the door handle told him that it was locked. He turned his attention to a gate in the iron railings that opened to the steps leading down to the basement and pushed against it. It resisted him. Loath to bring more pressure to bear and risk making a noise, he gripped the top of the gate and lifted it, easing the weight on its hinges and coaxing it open until he could step through.

Treading with care from step to step, he reached the tiny courtyard. Facing him was a window covered by a wrought iron grille. He peered through the bars. The inside of the window was covered by wooden shutters. To his right was a low door leading to the interior. Locked. George turned away and started to climb back up to the street.

As his foot met the second step, the front door opened wide. A broad shaft of light illuminated the area above him. Crouching low, he pressed himself against the damp stone steps, willing whoever was leaving the house not to look in his direction.

"Out with you, Titmus," said a voice from the doorway, followed by a loud miaow of complaint and the sound of the door shutting. George looked up cautiously. His gaze was met by a haughty look of contempt from a ginger tomcat who stood looking down at him for a moment before hissing and setting forth into the night. George took a moment to recover his composure. That voice. It was a woman's, not young by the sound of it. And the accent. He recalled the holidays he'd spent as a child with Aunt Minnie, who kept a boarding house in New Brighton. The accent was Merseyside, just like hers.

Back on the pavement, George was on the point of calling it a day. If the house had stood within the row of terraces, there would have been no point in persisting, but it was at the end. He turned the corner into the side street. A brick wall extended from the rear of the house, enclosing the back garden and running for some fifty feet until it met the side of another terrace of houses. Partway along was a solid timber door. He pushed. Bolted. Reaching up, he could grip the top of the wall without difficulty. He hoisted himself up until his eyes were above the top of the wall and peered into the space beyond. The area immediately below him was engulfed in darkness but, to his right, enough light shone from the house for him to see a bare flag-stoned yard leading to the back door of the building. Two windows on the ground floor glowed brightly. The curtains had not been drawn. The upper floors were dark.

George lowered himself back to the pavement. Just beyond the door in the wall, an overhanging branch provided a useful handhold, allowing him to pull himself up onto the wall and straddle it. He peeped through the branches to take a closer look at the house. The window near the back door revealed shelves with pots and pans and a plain deal table. A woman appeared with a kettle and filled it from a tap over the kitchen sink, then turned away and disappeared.

Through the other window, he saw a wall covered in floral wallpaper, a fireplace, and a picture in a gilt frame. He thought it must be the back parlour. His angle of observation was too acute to tell whether the room was occupied, but then Anthony Spencer himself appeared at the window and drew the curtains. The back yard was suddenly dark. Some light still shone from the kitchen, but the parlour window was obscured by heavy drapes, save for a narrow chink of light where the curtains had not been drawn to their full extent.

George was acutely aware that, despite the darkness, he was exposed to the gaze of any passer-by that might happen to look his way. So far, the street had remained empty, but at that moment, a man came around the corner with a large solid-looking dog on a leash.

He swung his right leg over the top of the wall and dropped into the darkness. To his relief, he landed on soft ground, a garden bed or vegetable patch. He heard the dog walker's footsteps coming closer. When they drew level, the dog gave out a low growl followed by loud sniffing and a high-pitched whine.

"What is it now, Dash?" its owner said irritably. The dog growled again, deep in the back of its throat. George stood still. His eyes were fixed on the house, expecting the back door to open at any moment.

"Damn it, Dash, that's enough. Come on with you now," said the man, raising his voice. The dog's feet scrabbled for purchase as it was dragged away, finally surrendering with a gruff woof of displeasure.

George wondered whether there was any point in continuing. Any hope of being able to learn what was happening inside the house had all but disappeared when the parlour curtains were drawn. But that remaining chink of light couldn't be ignored. He'd just have to get close enough to the window.

First things first. As he passed the garden door, he stopped and gently pulled back the two bolts. Reaching into his jacket, he retrieved his revolver and checked the five-shot chamber before returning it to his pocket.

He crept towards the parlour window. Anthony was seated with his back to him. George assumed that Figgis and O'Doyle were present in the room and also, perhaps, the woman he'd seen in the kitchen - whoever she might be. He'd try to get a proper glimpse inside to satisfy his curiosity, but his main objective was to hear what was being said and, for that, he'd have to put his ear to the glass. The curtains looked thick enough to ensure that he'd not be seen from within.

George drew closer and moved to his left to widen his angle of view through the gap in the curtains. He could see a seated figure who, according to Alfie's description, must be Figgis. The man's lips moved as he slammed his right fist repeatedly against the open palm of his left hand. Next to him, George could only see the skirt of a woman seated alongside him. O'Doyle was not in his field of vision, so he ducked beneath the windowsill and shuffled to his right to gain a view of the other side of the room. Straightening, he saw a figure sitting opposite Anthony in the far corner of the room. Not O'Doyle. Not a man. He'd seen her picture. The person that Verity had asked him to investigate before Lizzie's murder. The actress who'd disappeared. Cynthia Grant.

Dressed in a simple gingham frock with her hair drawn back, she sat with hunched shoulders, hands clasped on her lap. Eyes downcast. She was the object of Figgis's tirade, if that's what it was. As he watched, the woman who'd been sitting next to Figgis crossed the room. It was the woman from the kitchen. Her hair struck him first – red with streaks of grey – it fell wildly around her shoulders. The way she strode across the room gave the impression of barely restrained anger. Near fifty, he thought, with a solid, almost manly physique. With a sudden movement, she gripped Cynthia by the arm, hoisted her roughly to her feet, and marched her away. George was left with the image of Cynthia's face, eyes wide with fear and pain.

Anthony was speaking now, gesturing airily, addressing Figgis, who nodded his agreement. George inched forward, resting his hands on the windowsill. He rolled up his woollen cap and put an ear against the glass. A dull murmur was all he could hear. He pressed his ear more firmly to the window and covered his other ear with his hand. "… tomorrow Bert… first train… then to Larkford… I'll meet you… treat her…"

Figgis's response was inaudible. George strained his ears trying to pick up a word or two. It made the wailing screech behind him all the more startling. As his brain fought to settle his frayed nerves, a second unearthly sound, half an octave higher, assaulted his ears. Turning to face the source of the cacophony, he felt a surge of relief at the sight of Titmus, ginger fur standing on end, body arched, facing off at a chunky tortoiseshell interloper. The noise brought Anthony and Figgis to the window. They drew the curtains and laughed at the sight of the two feline antagonists. Then Anthony's expression changed as he caught sight of George edging his way past the cats towards the gate.

He heard shouting and looked towards the back door. There was movement in the kitchen. He raced for the door in the garden wall and wrenched it open. A final hurried glance behind showed a man emerging from the house. Anthony and Figgis still stood at the parlour window. His pursuer must be O'Doyle. He slammed the garden door behind him and sprinted back towards St Peter's Street.

Rounding the corner, he crouched down and looked back the way he'd come. The garden door was open and O'Doyle was standing there, looking around, uncertain which way to go. After a moment, he turned to his right, heading down the side street, away from George. Figgis appeared next and George ducked back when he looked in his direction. Had he been seen? There was no time to worry about that. He set off at a run towards Islington Green. After a few yards, hearing no sign of pursuit, he slowed to a walk and turned to look back. A hansom cab was the only thing in sight, approaching at a brisk trot.

He was about to hail it when O'Doyle appeared and turned in his direction, breaking into a run when he saw him. The cab was almost opposite him. If it stopped to pick him up, O'Doyle might be upon him before it could get going. O'Doyle's boots thudded on the pavement. The cab would soon be past him. George reached for his pistol. As he did so, the cab stopped and a hand reached out. "Run, Mister Benson, run. Get aboard," its occupant shouted as the cab driver twitched his whip over the horse's flank. O'Doyle picked up speed, drawing a blade from his coat.

George grabbed wildly for the outstretched arm, stumbling and almost crashing onto the road, then a brawny arm grasped him, and heaved him flat on his face onto the floor of the cab. The cabbie cracked his whip again and shouted at the horse to urge it on. O'Doyle's footsteps sounded right upon them and then, blessedly, grew fainter as George was borne along the road and around a corner, the cab not slowing until they were well away from the scene.

"That was a close one, guv," George scrambled up to sit next to his saviour.

"Dick. What on earth …?"

"Am I doing here? Alfie's idea. Thought you might need a bit of help if things turned awkward. Got that right, didn't he?"

"This cab. How …?"

"Save your breath, Mr Benson. The cab belongs to our Uncle Horace. Owes us a favour or two he does. Alfie borrowed it for the evening. That's him up top."

Safely deposited on his doorstep, George thought over the evening's events. The presence of Cynthia Grant at the house and the rough manner in which she'd been treated. That red-haired woman. He'd mentioned her to Dick.

"Oh, sounds like Ada, that does. The Archdeacon, they call her. A right terror, she is." Then there were the fragments of speech that he'd heard through the window, 'tomorrow Bert', then 'first train', Anthony said. Train to where? Then 'Larkford'. Was that a person? A place? He'd said he'd meet Bert. At Larkford, perhaps? And those last words, 'treat her'. Treat who? And how was this person to be treated? Was it Cynthia?

Sleep beckoned. Tomorrow, he had two new client appointments as well as some outstanding reports to write. After that, he'd consider what to do as a consequence of his adventure at the St Peter's Street address. Perhaps it would be best to write to Mortimer and Verity and suggest a meeting.

It was two days later, just after George had finished breakfast, that a loud rat-tat had him shuffling along his hallway to the front door.

The telegram was succinct.

COME TO THORNEYCROFT URGENT MORTIMER

Chapter 22

The carriage from Bicester station had barely come to a halt before Mortimer wrenched the door open and ushered him unceremoniously up the front steps.

Once inside, Mortimer led him into the library. Not a word was said, but Mortimer's grim expression warned George to prepare for disturbing news.

Verity was sitting at the table in the centre of the room. Next to her sat Ambrose, holding her hand and stroking it gently. George had never seen her like this. Hair hung about her face in loose strands, her red-rimmed eyes had a look of vacant despair. Mortimer pointed him to the nearest chair.

"Thank you, George, for getting here so quickly," Mortimer began, taking the chair next to him.

"It's Mary," whispered Verity.

"Yes, George," Mortimer said, "Mary has been abducted."

"What?"

"She…"

"Let me tell it, Mortimer," Verity withdrew her hand from Ambrose and tucked her wayward hair behind her ears.

"It happened the night before last, after the performance. We'd left the theatre, Mary and I. Our lodgings were not that far away and the streets were well lit. It was a woman, you see. We came upon her in the street. She appeared to have injured her leg. There she was sitting on a doorstep moaning and rubbing her ankle. Mary trotted over and asked if she needed help. I should have realised something wasn't quite right about her, I suppose, but hindsight's all very well.

"Anyway, she begged us to help her to her house. Weak and pleading. What else would any reasonable person do? 'It's just a street away. We can cut through the alley there. My son will be home soon, he'll tend to me', she said. So, Mary took one arm and I the other and raised her up. She put on quite an act, I must say, groaning and whimpering. Some passers-by stopped to see what the matter was, but left us to it once she was on her feet. Off we shuffled, along the alleyway. I didn't know where it led, just took her at her word. Halfway along she groaned and said she needed to rest and that's when it all went wrong."

Verity took a drink from a glass of water at her elbow. George saw a livid, dark bruise circling her wrist.

"There were two of them. A big, ugly brute blocked our path. I realised we'd been tricked and looked round, intending to retreat the way we'd come. The second man was right behind us. He wasn't a big fellow, but he took a firm grip on my wrist. It was his words that frightened me. 'Quiet now me darlin' or I'll cut yez, so I will', he said, and I'm sure he meant it.

"The woman had Mary by the hair and pushed her onto her knees. The poor girl tried to struggle, but in vain. The big man pulled a dirty handkerchief from his pocket and stuffed it into her mouth. It sickens me to think of it." She paused to take another drink of water.

"After the first shock of it, I somehow regained my composure. Something had to be done, so I did what young ladies do in penny dreadfuls. I swooned. You know, flopped down in a heap."

"You fainted?" said George.

"Of course, I didn't," Verity replied sharply, sounding more like her old self. "I pretended to faint. I didn't have a plan. It was just a way of preventing them from taking us further along the alley. Perhaps someone might come along and disturb them. It certainly caused consternation. The big man and the woman were still busy with Mary. They'd pulled her to her feet. I had my eyes almost shut, feigning unconsciousness, but could see their shapes in the darkness. 'This one's fainted,' the second man said. I thought he might try to help me up, more fool me. 'Stupid bitch,' he said and kicked me in the ribs."

"Damned blackguard," Ambrose said vehemently.

"Yes Ambrose, he was certainly no gentleman. The woman told him to get me on my feet and she didn't mince her words. He did as he was told. I still pretended to be unconscious; made myself a dead weight. He struggled and managed to prop me against a wall like a rag doll. As he took a step back, I drove a hatpin into his neck. That sent him staggering, and I took to my heels, screaming blue murder. I ran straight out into the road, yelling at the top of my voice."

"Good God," George exclaimed. "Then what happened?"

"It was late. There was no one about. I stood in the middle of the road, expecting one of them to come dashing out of the alley at any moment. A light went on in a house across the road and a man came to the door. Then more men came running around the corner. I tried to explain - 'my friend, in the alley, help, please help,' I wasn't at my most coherent. More people appeared. 'Come on, we've no time to waste,' I shouted and pointed towards the alley. 'There, down there.' Three or four of them went. I ran after them. There was nothing. The alley was empty except for poor Mary's hat lying in the mud. They'd gone and taken her with them." Verity fell silent. Retelling the painful events sapped her energy and her spirit. She put her head in her hands.

Mortimer took up the story. "The police were called George. They've taken a statement. I received a telegram from Verity yesterday and fetched her here. Then I summoned you. Who the devil are these people and what do they want with Mary? Verity is beside herself. We all are. George, we need to find them."

A few minutes later, George put up his hand to stem the barrage of questions directed at him. Verity had recovered and she and Mortimer vied with one another to quiz him as he revealed the fruits of his investigation into Anthony Spencer.

"Please, hold your horses. Let me recap," George pleaded. "Verity, you asked me to try to discover the whereabouts of Cynthia Grant after she disappeared. I drew a blank then and thought that was that. Then, after Lizzie James was killed you persuaded me, in your inimitable way, to investigate Anthony Spencer. What we now know is that Cynthia Grant is at that house in Islington. It's clear from what I saw that she was under duress. I'm satisfied that she's being held there against her will and that Anthony Spencer has her in his power. Why, is another question.

"Then we have Spencer's association with this Bishopsgate Mob. Why on earth would a celebrated impresario, a man who mixes in high society, be involved with common criminals? Your assailants, Verity, were the very people present with Anthony Spencer at the Islington House. Their names are Bert Figgis, he's the big one, Jackie O'Doyle is the charmer who had hold of you, and the woman's name is Ada Cole. The snippets of conversation I heard there may be our strongest clue as to Mary's whereabouts. The more I think about it, the more convinced I am that the name Larkford is the key. They've taken her to Larkford, though whether that is the name of a person or a place, I can't say. A place seems more likely. There, that's it."

"Might they not have taken her to that house in Islington, though?" Mortimer asked. "Since they're keeping Cynthia at that address."

George considered the question. "I can't rule that out, Mortimer, but Anthony said that he would meet them at Larkford, or at least that's what I believe, based on the fragments that I managed to hear. However, I take your point. Verity, what do you think?"

"Oh… yes, I suppose we must consider both possibilities. I have a different point to make."

"Yes?"

"Mary was not the intended victim of this abduction. I was. It all comes back to the blackmail attempt. Cynthia was the original blackmailer. She disappeared and is now Anthony Spencer's prisoner. Lizzie tried in her rather gauche way to pick up where Cynthia left off and was murdered. And someone tried to lay their hands on the blackmail material by searching Lizzie's room, not knowing that I had taken it.

"But then I advertised the fact that I had it by introducing new lines into the play. Anthony was not present for that performance, but he would have heard about it. He'll be livid that I escaped, but he has Mary, and I've no doubt that the price for her release will involve that envelope of incriminating material. Mind you, all it said about him is that he's not all he seems. There's nothing specifically damning in there. But perhaps it's what he imagines it to contain that is driving him."

Mortimer was about to speak when Ambrose piped up.

"I've never met this Anthony Spencer, but he's obviously a thoroughly bad lot. I can understand that he'd be keen to get his hands on that envelope, but I fear he might go further than that. If he was behind that girl Lizzie's demise, what's to say that he wouldn't be prepared to eliminate you, Verity, or Mary now that he's got her? It's what may lie in your heads as much as what he imagines the envelope to contain that will concern him."

"If that's the case, you can add Cynthia to the list," Verity responded. "She's the one who intended to blackmail him in the first place. The irony is that I have no idea what Cynthia had discovered about him that would lay him open to blackmail."

"Very well," Mortimer said, rising to his feet. "We've heard from George, and we're all now aware that Anthony Spencer is behind Mary's abduction. The question is what should we - indeed, what can we do to secure her safe release?"

"And bring Spencer and his gang of felons to book," added Ambrose.

"Well, at the risk of incurring Verity's displeasure, we could leave it to the police," George ventured.

Verity's response was precisely what he'd expected. "Thank you for that, George. I'll simply say that if the way the police dealt with Lizzie's death is anything to go by, then poor Mary is lost. I have provided them with a statement and they will do as they see fit. However, I'll not rest until Mary is back among us. Is that sufficiently clear for you, George?"

"Perfectly. Then we should agree on a course of action."

"Of course, we must," Verity said exasperatedly. "Am I the only one here who fully grasps the need for urgency? At this very moment, Mary is being subjected to heaven knows what at the hands of these monsters?"

"Yes, of course," said Mortimer, "but what options do we have? If, as George believes, Mary is being held at a place called Larkford, how do we find it? It's not a place I've heard of. Do any of …? Yes, Ambrose?"

"Well, Mortimer," Ambrose said, moving to the bookshelves lined around the walls, "perhaps the answer is at hand. Now let me see, do you have a gazetteer?"

"I don't know?"

"Yes, of course we do." Verity rose and walked to the far corner of the library. "Here, this is it, Bartholomew's Gazetteer of the British Isles. Come on Mortie, lend a hand."

Mortimer brought the heavy volume over to the table.

"Now, then." Verity leafed briskly through the pages. "Here are the Ls. La, Lar… Lark. We have Larkfield. There are three entries with that name and then… voila. Here it is, Larkford. Larkford Grange, in fact, which Bartholomew describes as a country seat, one mile northeast of Beachcott

St James," Verity exclaimed triumphantly. "Strange, isn't it? That would only be some ten miles from here, yet I've not heard of it. Have you, Mortie?"

He shook his head. "Can't say I have."

"Bravo, Verity," Ambrose banged his fist on the table. "Now, we have the fox's lair. Time to set the hounds on him. What say you, Mortimer?"

Ambrose's call to arms was interrupted by a knock on the library door, which opened to reveal Mrs Cooper, the housekeeper. "Forgive the interruption, Sir Mortimer, but I have a gentleman at the door wishing to see you and Miss Verity. He says it's a most urgent matter. I have his card," she said, indicating the silver salver in her hand.

"Thank you, Mrs Cooper." Mortimer took the card from her. "My word. It's Phillip Aspinall."

Chapter 23

Phillip cut a dejected figure as Mrs Cooper showed him into the library. He stood in the doorway, blinking uncertainly under the gaze of the room's occupants.

"Mr Aspinall, do come in," Mortimer said kindly, offering his hand. He'd only met Phillip once before when he'd visited Verity in Cheltenham. Then, Phillip had been full of himself on the strength of the play's success. Now, he was diminished, in body and in spirit.

Verity took Phillip by the arm, offering him a seat at the table. He shuffled and slumped in his seat. She sat next to him and took his hand. "Phillip, you remember my brother, Mortimer, don't you?" Phillip darted a glance in Mortimer's direction and nodded. "These other gentlemen are my uncle, Mr Ambrose Mallard and Mr George Benson."

Mortimer placed a glass of brandy on the table. "Mr Aspinall, you're among friends here. We're all coming to terms with the awful events in Coventry. Please take a drink and tell us what we can do to help you."

Phillip whispered a barely audible 'thank you,' and reached for the glass. His hand trembled as he raised it to his lips and sipped the bracing liquid. He sat silently contemplating the glass in his hand, then took another sip and put the glass back on the table.

"Thank you," Phillip repeated, his voice still weak but gaining in strength. "Please forgive my presumption in coming here. This has left me in a terrible predicament. As the play's director, I have a responsibility for the company, and now I have lost three of them. Anthony Spencer has cut us all adrift, you know. The tour is finished. We are wound up. Left high and dry."

"Have you seen Anthony?" Verity said.

"No. He sent a telegram. Didn't have the decency to tell me face to face. Of course, I knew that the tour was finished. How could we carry on under the circumstances? It's just that he left me to break the news to the company. You can imagine how they all took it. They don't even know if they'll be paid for the last few performances. I couldn't bear it any longer. But, Verity, what's become of Mary? I know what you told the police – an abduction? Why on earth would anyone do such a thing? Anyway, I was in such a state of mind - the only thing I could think of was to come to you. I must beg your pardon, Sir Mortimer. It was presumptuous of me to arrive without an invitation."

"Think nothing of it, Mr Aspinall – Phillip. And do call me Mortimer. You are most welcome to stay here for the present. Do you have any luggage, by the way?"

"An overnight bag. I sent my trunk back to London."

"Very well. Now, Phillip, let me introduce you to George Benson and Ambrose Mallard. George is a private investigator from London, and Ambrose is my late father's cousin." There was an exchange of nods. "Before I go any further. I must have a private word with Verity and George. I'm sure you understand. Ambrose, would you be so good as to take Phillip out onto the terrace? The afternoon is quite mild."

"Come along, old chap. Let me show you the vista. The view of the gardens and the lake has a decidedly calming effect, I find," Ambrose said, accompanying Phillip out of the library.

"Well, that was most unexpected," Mortimer said. "What are we going to do with Phillip Aspinall? I mean, here we are hatching a plan to rescue Mary and he turns up. It does rather complicate things."

"Quite so," George agreed, "and Phillip was one of the blackmail victims. According to your theory, he could still be Lizzie's murderer, couldn't he, Verity?"

"Oh, I don't believe I was ever truly convinced that Phillip could have done so. She was his niece, after all, and if I'm any judge of character, the man simply doesn't have it in him. I'm more than a little surprised that he'd be capable of bigamy, for that matter. No, George, Anthony Spencer is the villain here. He and his criminal associates."

"I think that is the inescapable conclusion, Verity," replied George. "So, do we take Phillip into our confidence? We don't have the luxury of delaying our plans, waiting for Phillip to recover and go on to London. What's your opinion, Mortimer?"

"He just might have something to contribute. He's known Anthony Spencer for several years, I understand. Let's at least share with him the fact that we know that Spencer is behind Mary's abduction and Cynthia's disappearance, too, in all probability. The murder remains a matter of speculation, so we should stay silent on that subject. Let's see what he has to say for himself. It might prove enlightening. Are we agreed?"

Verity and George nodded.

Phillip did as he was asked and sat quietly while George recounted how he'd observed the house in St Peter's Street and discovered Cynthia Grant being held prisoner by Anthony and his accomplices, the Bishopsgate Mob. He blinked, his face a picture of confusion and shock.

Verity followed with her account of the abduction and the revelation that her assailants were the very same crew of felons. Phillip shook his head.

"Phillip," Verity continued, "what we're about to tell you must not be divulged to anyone. We have discussed whether to include you in our deliberations regarding what we must do to help Mary. And we believe that you can be trusted to keep a confidence. Is our trust well placed?"

"Oh – well, if what you tell me is intended to help Mary, then yes - yes, it is."

"Does Anthony Spencer have a house in the country, Phillip?"

"I've heard him mention that he had a bolthole, as he called it. I never learned where, though."

"It might surprise you to learn that it's not far from here. A place called Larkford Grange. Doesn't ring a bell?"

"No, I've not heard of it."

"Well, we believe that's where Mary's being held. And when you arrived, we were about to decide how to rescue her."

"But surely, if you know where she is, the police—"

"No police," Verity snapped. "I have no confidence in the police. When we have Mary safe and sound, then they can bring her kidnappers before the courts."

"But they—"

"Phillip!" Verity interrupted. "Ask yourself what the police would be obliged to do if they were to learn that you had one wife in Wimbledon and another in Epping?"

Phillip looked aghast.

"I'm sorry if that seems brutal, Phillip, but we are in deadly earnest here, no pun intended."

Phillip bristled. "You asked me if I was to be trusted. Now, I would ask the same of you. I will play my part in helping to secure Mary's release, but I must have your assurance that my personal… arrangements are not disclosed."

"Of course, let's agree that the police need not be inconvenienced on either account," Verity said with a smile.

"Phillip," Mortimer said, "you have had a professional relationship with Anthony Spencer for some time, have you not?"

"On and off, over the past ten years. I acted in productions of his to begin with. As a director, this was the third time that I've worked with him."

"And you had no inkling that he might be capable of criminal acts?"

Phillip hesitated. "Criminal acts? Nothing like abduction, absolutely not. But I have suspected for some time that his so-called success as an impresario is more gloss than substance. Oh, he plays the part very well. Loves the romance of the theatre and cutting a figure in society. But I know that some of his productions have been less than successful commercially. I'm at a loss to know how he found financial backing for The Importance of Being Earnest, in fact."

"Really," Mortimer remarked. "Might that account for his criminal associations? Is he resorting to crime to finance his theatrical career?"

"Or is the theatre purely a facade for criminal activity?" George chipped in.

"Gentlemen," Verity interjected, "there'll be time enough for such conjecture when we have rescued Mary. Now, to business. We must have a plan of action before dinner."

Chapter 24

That night, Verity sat at her dressing table, brushing her hair absent-mindedly. Her reflection gazed back at her, the frown lines on her forehead accentuated by the flickering firelight from the grate.

Throughout the tumultuous events of the past few months: the Henry Powell business, her sudden acting 'career,' even Lizzie's murder, she'd maintained a detached, clinical state of mind. Her natural inclination was to take control of events, but those few minutes in a noisome alleyway in Coventry had left their mark. The anxiety she felt now was disturbingly unfamiliar. Quite unlike her grief at the death of her parents, which was the only other deeply negative emotion she'd experienced.

Mary's abduction, she realised, was entirely due to her stubborn determination to pursue her own notions of justice. Her obsessive quest to pursue Lizzie's murderer, by making herself a target, was all well and good, but she'd also placed her dear friend in jeopardy.

***

Mortimer paced back and forth in the library. He thought back to the death of his father and the sudden adjustment he had to make to his life, in succeeding to the baronetcy. He'd felt indignant at the prospect of living in the country, managing the estate and leaving behind the pleasures and diversions of the city. But now, he fervently wished for the dull, measured existence that he'd resented so much.

Verity was his sister, friend, and confidante, but also his nemesis. He'd always humoured her, tolerated her enthusiasms and passions and, it must be said, allowed her to dominate him. It had simply seemed easier that way. He had the death of Henry Powell on his conscience as a consequence. A wicked man, to be sure. And not just Henry, either, but that was another story. The mantle of executioner sat heavily upon him. A mantle he'd never have sought of his own volition. Verity bestowed it on him. Now, she'd introduced a new peril into their lives and yet he could conceive of no other course than to follow and support her.

***

George stood at the lake's edge. The full moon rippled on the surface as a light breeze blew across the water. He too felt entangled in Verity's web. But for George Benson, the situation called for action rather than regret. Part of him relished the prospect of confronting the kidnappers. Despite Verity's display of bravado in urging him and her brother to rescue Mary, they would both rely on him in order to pull it off. So be it, he thought, harking back to his time as a Pinkerton agent. He'd risked his life then, helping to bring outlaws to justice, but Pinkerton's inglorious role as strike-breakers had caused him to doubt his employer's ethics and to part company with them.

Well, there was no doubt in his mind now. Where Anthony Spencer and those dregs of the East End were concerned, he'd do whatever was necessary to confound them. But in his own way. Verity's impetuousness could all too easily lead to disaster. He would do his darnedest to keep her in check.

***

The lantern in Ambrose's hand illuminated the nooks and crannies of the attic and the disorderly assortment of objects deposited there, from the domestic to the wildly exotic. It was his domain, and he delighted in its variety and the opportunity to lose himself, rummaging about and imagining the history behind each object. He'd sometimes carry away the treasures which had the greatest influence on his imagination, to contemplate them in the comfort of his room. A dusty antique globe, a rustic hobby horse with a few remaining strands of horsehair for a mane, and a battered ship's telescope were among his most prized finds. As Ambrose picked his way through the clutter, he noticed a pair of objects which, at first sight, looked ordinary but, on closer inspection, were anything but. Chuckling quietly to himself, Ambrose picked them up and went back downstairs.

***

Phillip lay on the bed, gazing dully at the ceiling in the semi-darkness. His world lay in ruins. The tour that held so much promise was over; his career with it, in all probability. In truth, he'd regarded Lizzie as an inconvenient and ungrateful liability. He'd taken her reluctantly under his wing when her widowed mother succumbed to consumption and look at how she'd repaid him, threatening to expose his bigamy. It was comical, really, the way she'd tried to appear threatening. He'd seen right through her, of course. She admitted that it was Cynthia who'd involved her in blackmail to begin with, but she'd died before he could persuade her to reveal the evidence on which Cynthia's extortion attempt was founded. Cynthia was a different matter. He didn't doubt that she would have made good on her threats to expose him. When she disappeared, he couldn't believe his luck, despite the difficulty it caused him in losing a vital member of the cast.

Now, he may as well be avenged on Anthony. If my career's over, then I'll take him down too, he thought. There was some satisfaction in that notion. Vengeance was such a theatrical emotion and Phillip was a man of the theatre.

***

Meanwhile, a few miles away, Mary crouched miserably, shivering in the dark.

Chapter 25

"Thank you, Janet," said Verity, as her maid placed a tea tray on the library table. "That will be all for the present."

While Verity occupied herself with pouring tea and handing cups around, George stood at a blackboard and easel which had been found at the back of a cupboard in what had once been Mortimer and Verity's nursery-cum-schoolroom.

Mortimer, Ambrose and Phillip sat at the table and, having dispensed the tea, Verity joined them.

"We've all had time to sleep on it," George began, "so allow me to outline the plan I've devised."

"One moment," Ambrose reached inside his jacket, producing a conductor's baton. "Found it in the attic, George. Thought you could use it as a pointer. It provides a certain gravitas, don't you think?"

George couldn't help but smile. "Thank you, Ambrose. It's just the thing."

"First," George continued, "we need to know the exact location of Larkford Grange."

"Yes," Mortimer said, producing a folded map and spreading it out on the table. "I managed to find this Ordnance Survey County Map. We know from the Gazetteer that Larkford Grange is just a mile northeast of Beachcott St. James and here it is, you see." He placed his finger on the map. "Now, Verity, you recall that neither of us had heard of it. Well, I mentioned the name to Clough just this morning and now I understand why. We would know it as the Norrington House."

"The Norrington House?" Verity echoed. "Yes, now I remember. It would be about twenty years ago. We were just children. There was such a scandal. Colonel Norrington shot his wife and her lover and then jumped off the roof. The county spoke of little else for weeks."

"That's right. According to Clough, the house remained empty for several years but 'some gentleman from London', as he put it, bought it eighteen months ago."

George bent over the map. "Just trying to get the lie of the land. The road from Beachcott St. James passes quite close to the house. There's an extensive area of woodland to the west of it and a ridge to the southeast. That could make a good observation point if it's not too exposed."

Returning to the blackboard, he tapped it with the baton. "Now that we have an initial idea of the terrain, the next step is to get a first-hand view of the place."

"A scouting mission, is that it?" Ambrose said eagerly.

"Precisely, Ambrose. A reconnaissance. We must try to establish who is there and how we can best gain entry to the house. And it must be done soon. Tomorrow."

Mortimer nodded, "Yes, of course. That will be a job for you and me, George."

"Hmm. I've given that some thought, Mortimer, and I'd say yes if it were not for one thing. You've met Anthony Spencer. Only once I grant you, but if you were spotted, it could give the game away. I will go alone."

"But didn't Anthony and his ruffians see you in the garden of that house?" Mortimer countered.

"It was dark and all they'd have seen was my back as I got the deuce out of there. I'll be dressed as a farm labourer, Mortimer."

"That's well and good, George, but have you thought it through?" Verity said dismissively.

"Of course, I've thought it through. You must see my point, surely?" George answered curtly.

"Yes, George, mere woman as I am," Verity replied, with what she considered just the right note of sarcasm, "I do see your point about not being recognised but have you considered how you'll travel to Larkford Grange?"

"Yes, Verity, I was coming to that. That old cart next to the stables. We could load it up with some hay or milk churns, anything agricultural to help me to look the part. I'd drive over on that."

"Bravo, George, ingenious. And what will you do with the cart while you carry out your reconnaissance? You can't very well park it outside the gates and leave the horse to its own devices, you know. Someone must accompany you and take care of it while you go about your business."

"Aha, and that someone will be me," Ambrose cried, jumping to his feet.

"But—" George began.

"No buts old chap. There's no other choice. I'm the only one here who's not known to this Spencer fellow apart from your good self. Now, I know what you're thinking. Ambrose is just a silly old beggar who'll be more of a hindrance than a help, but you'd be surprised by what I'm capable of. Some of my escapades out in India would make your hair curl, and no mistake. Why, I—"

"Yes, yes, Ambrose," Verity interrupted, "you can regale George with your adventures another time. But he's right, George. Ambrose is the only choice. Now, tell us what comes next after you've discovered the disposition of the enemy."

George took a deep breath and exhaled, conceding inwardly that he'd been outmanoeuvred.

"That will depend on what I find, but the short answer is that we will need to be prepared to enter the house and free Mary. Unless we are very fortunate, that will mean the use of force to overcome her captors and that, as my old army training tells me, requires reinforcements. You sent the telegram, Mortimer?"

"Yes, I popped over to Flaxminton after breakfast."

"Good, then tomorrow afternoon you can expect my two associates, the redoubtable Cotton brothers, Alfie and Dick."

Chapter 26

The clouds parted as Lancelot, the shire horse, trudged past the parish church on the outskirts of Beachcott St. James. George held the reins and nudged Ambrose with his elbow to wake him for the fifth time since they'd set off shortly before dawn. Ambrose grunted, then snored on. A sudden shower had left them feeling damp and uncomfortable, but now a glimpse of sunlight offered some small comfort and stimulated the bird life, with the trills of a mounting morning chorus accompanied by the monotonous cooing of a wood pigeon.

Their first glimpse of Larkford Grange came as they rounded a bend, where the road ahead descended gradually to flatten out and run straight on for a half-mile. From their elevated position, the roof and its sprinkling of chimneys were visible beyond a copse of trees.

George craned his neck to see above the hedgerow. The house gradually revealed itself. It looked older than George had imagined. Red brick and half-timbered walls spoke of a substantial manor house rather than a grand country seat. The structure had two main storeys surmounted by gabled attics and comprised two wings on either side of a central section. Beyond the west wing were stables. And beyond them, a thick belt of trees and shrubs extended for some distance with open pasture after that.

As the cart approached a pair of tall brick pillars flanking the main gate to the estate, George spied the ridge he'd noted on Mortimer's map, off to the right of the house. Nestled below it was a modest whitewashed cottage.

They drew level with the gateway and George glanced along the drive to the house, looking for signs of habitation. Aside from a column of smoke rising from one of the chimneys, there was nothing.

Ambrose's head lolled with the rhythmic movement of the cart, but George let him sleep until they'd rounded the next bend. Here, the road widened and a flat open space fronting a rickety farm gate offered just enough room to draw up off the road. The gate had settled into the ground and its dilapidated appearance gave George some confidence that it had not been in use for years. He could leave Ambrose here without risking some local farmer coming along and demanding access to his fields. Lancelot put his head down and grazed on a tussock of long grass.

"Ambrose, wake-up," he urged, shaking his companion gently."

"Uh?" Ambrose muttered. "Here, are we?" He rubbed his eyes and stretched. "Hope that sun stays out, old chap. Need to get the chill out of my bones."

"We've just passed the house, Ambrose. I want you to wait here until I return. Just stay with the cart. That's all you need to do. Understood?"

"Perfectly. Old Lancelot and I will just stay put and pass the time of day. Don't suppose you can say how long you'll be?"

"Just long enough to get a closer look at the house and see what's going on there. A couple of hours, perhaps. Just stay put."

"Stay put, absolutely. Now get along with you."

George jumped down. Mortimer had supplied the two of them with an assortment of old clothes to give them the appearance of a couple of country labouring types. George wore a collarless, coarse flannel shirt with a dark woollen muffler under a stained buff waistcoat. An old tweed jacket with leather patches on the elbows and trousers in the same material completed the ensemble, together with leather gaiters around his calves and a grey cloth cap. Ambrose had taken a fancy to a shepherd's smock, and a broad brimmed straw hat. All he needed, George thought, was a piece of straw between his teeth to give a passable impression of a village idiot.

He set off briskly, back the way they'd come and passed the main gate without a sideways glance, giving the impression of a man intent on going about his business. He'd noticed from the cart that further on there was a stile in a gap in the hedge and reasoned that would give him access to a footpath running along the boundary of the estate. From there, he could reach the ridge of high ground overlooking the house.

To George's relief, they'd seen hardly a soul on the way over from Thorneycroft. Keen not to draw attention to himself, he'd almost reached the stile when the sound of hooves on the road alerted him to an approaching rider. He pulled his cap down and hunched his shoulders.

Peeping out under the peak, George saw the rider approach. The straight back, elbows in, heels down, and the crisp trot of a well-schooled mount reminded him of the cavalry officers he'd seen in his army days. Although he was dressed in finely tailored civilian riding garb, the military bearing of the rider was evident from the man's monocle, clipped moustache and equally clipped greeting as he drew level.

"Good morning, my man. Fine day."

George muttered a "Good morning, sir," in what he hoped would pass for a rural accent, and kept on walking. Anxious to avoid a conversation with the horseman, he kept his head down and walked on. The clip-clop stopped abruptly, and the horse snorted as it was pulled up. George stiffened, waiting for the man to call after him, sensing the fellow's eyes on his back. He was almost at the stile but dared not climb over it while being observed. He kept moving until he heard the horse resume its trot, the hoof beats fading as it passed down the road.

George hazarded a look behind and stayed close to the hedge, watching until the rider passed the entrance to Larkford Grange. Whoever the man was, at least he was not associated with the occupants of the house. Reassured, George retraced his steps and climbed swiftly over the stile, striking out along a rough path toward the ridge.

The path ran straight ahead, rising with the contours of the land. To his left, a dry-stone wall marked the boundary with the Grange, while on the right, a broad open field sloped away to a hedge some two hundred yards away. In the distance, he could see the spire of the church they'd passed.

He kept to the right of the path and away from the wall so that his head would not be visible to anyone looking from the house. When he thought that he was level with the highest point of the ridge, he removed his cap and crouched behind the wall, then straightened until he could see above it.

The house was hidden behind the ridge, with only some wisps of rising smoke to indicate its position. George found a toehold and hoisted himself up, his thoughts straying to the last time he'd scaled a wall. This time he'd have to make damned sure he wasn't discovered. There'd be no passing hansom cab to save him.

On the other side, he stayed low and made his way towards the edge of the ridge. The rough grass was damp from an earlier shower. A few patches of gorse provided the only cover and it was behind one of them that George knelt to look down at the house. He still could only see the upper floors and the roof. Cautiously, he moved forward on all fours, feeling the dampness under his palms and soaking into the knees of his trousers. At the very edge, he lay flat on his stomach. This vantage point gave him a clear view of the front of the house and the east wing.

The sky was almost clear of clouds and the sun provided some welcome warmth on his back. Fifteen minutes passed, with no signs of life. George took a small pair of field glasses from his coat pocket and scanned the nearest windows. The nearest ground floor room at the front of the east wing looked like a sitting room. He could make out the back of a sofa and a potted plant on a table next to it, but that was all. The room above it had curtains which, although open, obscured most of the interior. Adjusting the focus of his binoculars, he thought he could see a wardrobe and one corner of a fourposter. Along the side of the building, there were several windows on both the ground and first floors, but his angle of observation was too acute to see into the rooms beyond.

He was wondering how he might get closer to the house when he heard it. The steady crunching of the gravel along the drive had him traversing the binoculars to his left. The carriage had covered a third of the distance from the entrance gate to the house. As it drew closer, he could see a woman's bonnet through the carriage window sitting facing forward and beyond her another head. A man's.

He shifted his view to the front door. The visitors were expected, for there at the open door stood Anthony Spencer, dressed in a tweed suit, very much the country squire. Next to him was the bulky figure of Bert Figgis, leaning on the stick with a brass handle that Alfie had described to him. 'Calls it his staff of office', Alfie had told him. To George, it looked more like a fancy cudgel. The carriage came to a stop, and another figure emerged from the house. There was no mistaking Ada's long mane of red and grey. She bustled up to the carriage door and extended a hand to help the female passenger out, then enveloped her in a hug and took her towards the house. The visitor stopped briefly and untied her bonnet, shaking her hair loose with one hand. The resemblance was striking. There stood a younger and slighter version of Ada Cole. From the carriage's other side, a man, silver-haired and walking with a slight stoop, came into view. He nodded to Anthony and went into the house.

The carriage driver got down and took hold of two items of luggage from within, then carried them inside. Emerging soon after, he drove the carriage away towards the stables. Bert Figgis and Anthony exchanged a few words, then turned and went inside.

George pondered the arrival of these two visitors. He had no idea who the elderly man could be. He certainly didn't look like a member of the Bishopsgate Mob. The woman intrigued him. Her resemblance to Ada Cole was so striking that there had to be a familial link. They could be sisters.

Thus far, he'd confirmed the presence of six people at Larkford Grange: Anthony Spencer, Bert Figgis, Ada Cole and the two new arrivals who, given that they had brought luggage, must have come to stay. Then there was the coachman. If Jackie O'Doyle was there, he'd not put in an appearance and George had seen no sign that Mary was at the house. He must get a closer look. There was no way that he could approach the front of the house without the considerable risk of being seen. An approach from the rear might be possible, although he had no idea as to the lie of the land in that direction. He'd have to move off to his right and work his way around to get a better view.

He'd started to move back from the edge of the ridge when he detected movement from the house. George pressed himself back into the grass. There were three of them. They'd come from the back of the house, walking along a gravel path in his direction. Ada and her sister, if that was their relationship, carried a large wicker basket between them, chattering companionably. Two paces behind them came Jackie O'Doyle, swinging a bunch of keys and whistling.

It was only after they'd passed directly beneath him that he realised where they were going. The cottage, nestled as it was at the foot of the ridge, was only twenty yards away to his left. He rolled over in that direction, keeping low until he could see it, a single-storey building of rough whitewashed stone and a slate roof covered with moss and lichen. The grassy slope of the ridge beneath him ran down almost to its back door, leaving only a small patch of garden overrun with weeds. The trio reached the front of the building and disappeared. Creaking hinges suggested that they must have gone inside.

George scrambled down the slope to the rear of the cottage. There were two windows at the back, covered by wooden shutters. He pressed his ear to one and heard nothing. Outside the second window, he listened again. Nothing at first but then a cry, a woman's voice raised in surprise. Or was it alarm? He listened harder and heard a man's voice raised in mocking laughter and then a confusion of several voices, but try as he might, he couldn't make out the words.

George rounded the corner to the end wall. There were no windows there. A few steps further took him to the next corner. He stopped and cautiously craned his neck to look along the front of the cottage, ready to duck back if anyone emerged. From this angle, he could see that there were two windows, shuttered like those at the rear, and between them the front door, which was closed. He resisted an urge to listen at the nearest window. He'd be too exposed to view from the house and to the risk of discovery if anyone emerged from the cottage.

Just as well. The clattering of the latch warned him. O'Doyle came out first, followed by the unknown woman. They stood on the threshold talking to someone inside.

"Well," said Jackie, "weren't those two surprised to see you? Their faces were a picture, were they not?"

"They look quite different to the last time I saw either of them," the woman said. "You've put the fear of God into them, Jackie," she laughed. *That accent*, George said to himself, *Merseyside, just like Ada's.*

"Aye, they're scared right enough, Ingrid, but it's yer sister that they're afeared of. Isn't that right, Ada?"

George could just see Ada in profile, standing in the doorway.

"And, they've got every reason to be scared," Ada said, "I've already broken Cynthia and that little Miss Mary is just starting to realise what a stew she's in. I'll have her begging me for mercy in no time."

"And what's to be done about Verity Mallard?" Ingrid asked.

"Ah, well, that was a bit of bad luck, so it was," Jackie said, rubbing the side of his neck. "She'll regret it all right. Nobody stabs me and gets away with it. When we do get her, she'll wish she was dead."

"Anthony said the same," Ingrid agreed. "I told him she'd gone off with her brother. Turns out his place is just a few miles from here."

"Aye, it is so, and she'll have no idea that we are coming for her. A couple of days, that's all. Then we send the three of them on their way. A nice sea voyage. Ada thinks it's a grand idea, don't yer Ada?"

"Three English women and ladies to boot. Oh, they'll fetch a pretty penny," Ada laughed. "Anyway, can't stop here talking. We've got some lessons to teach Miss Mary. It's only fair to let her know what she's in for. You get off now, Ingrid, and I'll talk to you later. Right then Jackie, let's get on with it." Jackie followed her inside and slammed the door behind him. Ingrid walked away towards the house.

George stood with his back against the cottage wall, thinking hard. He'd guessed correctly. The female visitor was Ada's sister. But more than that, she was Ingrid Lloyd. George knew the names of all the cast members, but although Verity had aired her suspicions about the blackmail victims, she'd only mentioned Ingrid in passing.

There'd been nothing to suggest that she was mixed up in this business.

And Verity was right - she was the target of that abduction in Coventry, not poor Mary. Jackie said they still intended to seize her. George considered his options. His aim had been to discover if Mary was at the Grange and he'd done that. What's more, he knew exactly where she was being kept. Not at the house itself, but at this cottage. And not just Mary, but Cynthia too. He felt the weight of his revolver in his pocket. He'd have the element of surprise on his side. But Jackie didn't strike him as the sort to be cowed by the sight of his gun, nor Ada for that matter. And even if he could get the captives out of there, how could he hope to get both of them away without detection and pursuit? He'd never get them to scramble back up the ridge and the only other option would be a dash across open ground to the main gate. That would be folly. They'd be in plain sight from the house. In any case, a farm cart pulled by an ageing shire horse offered no chance of getting safely away.

He moved away carefully, retracing his steps to the rear of the cottage, and clambered back up the ridge.

Ambrose stood, stroking Lancelot's great head as George arrived back at the cart. "Ah, there you are. We were just wondering whether you'd come to grief, weren't we old chap," he said, patting the horse's shoulder.

"I thought you might have fallen asleep again," George replied. "Did anyone bother you?"

"Bother me? No, hardly saw a soul. Had a pleasant chat with a fellow riding by, that's all."

"You what? For heaven's sake, Ambrose, the whole point in dressing like a couple of yokels was not to draw attention to ourselves. And you go and have a chat. He'd know immediately that you were no farm labourer."

"Well, if someone gives you the time of day, it's only common courtesy to respond in kind."

George sighed. "Was it a military-looking man? He'd have ridden past a few minutes after I left."

"Yes, that's the fellow. Major Hinton-Brown, late of the Indian Army. Very pleasant chap. Turns out we were both in Bangalore at the same time."

"And did this Major Hinton-Brown ask what you were doing dressed like a son of the soil but sounding like the lord of the manor?"

"No, can't say he did. But that's just good manners. A gentleman would not pry into the affairs of another."

"Let's get moving," George muttered wearily, climbing up into the driver's seat. Ambrose shrugged and got up alongside. George manoeuvred the cart with some difficulty until it was facing back towards Beachcott St. James. As they passed the Grange once more, his eyes were drawn to the cottage. He shuddered at the thought of what might be happening under its roof.

George satisfied Ambrose's curiosity as they made their way back. His companion listened quietly and, unusually, held his peace.

Chapter 27

It was almost noon when they arrived at Thorneycroft. Having changed their clothes, George and Ambrose joined Mortimer, Verity and Phillip at luncheon.

"Well, there you are then," Verity said. "I told you that I was their intended victim. What was it that woman, Ada, said? Three English women, fetching a pretty penny. My God, Mortimer, George - do they intend to sell us off to some… harem or bordello? I can't believe that such a thing could happen in this day and age. You know, it's ironic, but I used the prospect of such a thing to scare Lizzie, little thinking that such an outlandish notion could possibly be a reality. It's positively… gothic."

"And you heard them say that they would take Verity in a couple of days, George?" Mortimer said. "These rogues would dare to come here to Thorneycroft?"

"That's what O'Doyle was implying, I'm sure of it."

"And Ingrid," Verity said. "I'd no inkling that she was tied up in this. I'm astonished. Ada's sister, you say?"

"That's right. The resemblance was obvious if you saw them together," George confirmed.

"It certainly wasn't obvious when I encountered Ada in Coventry, but then it was dark and she had a bonnet covering her hair. And you said she had a male companion with her in the carriage? Describe him to me again, would you?"

George did so.

"Ha. That's one of the old stagers. What do you think, Phillip?"

Phillip Aspinall thought for a moment. He'd recovered his spirits since his arrival at Thorneycroft and looked and sounded more himself. "That's Sidney Fuller. I'm as surprised as you, Verity. Ingrid and Sidney. They're better actors than I thought."

"Thank you, George," Mortimer said. "Thank you for the information you've gathered and at considerable danger to yourself, I might add."

"Yes, thank you, George," Verity echoed.

George nodded, "I only wish I'd been able to get Mary away from there. Cynthia too, for that matter. It pains me more than I can say to think of them in that cottage, subject to the tender mercies of Ada and Jackie."

"Then it's time we stopped talking and took action."

Everyone turned to look at Ambrose. His voice had a hard edge, quite unlike his usual, affable self. "We have no time to lose," he continued. "We must free them now, today. We cannot allow those two ladies to suffer at their hands for a moment longer and we must forestall their nefarious plan to abduct you, Verity. George, your two associates will arrive shortly?"

"Yes, they telegraphed to say that they'd arrive at Bicester station at ten past two. That's in five minutes," George confirmed, consulting his pocket watch.

"Higgins is waiting for them. They should be here by three thirty," Mortimer added.

"Good, that will make five of us. How many did you say we'd be up against George?" Mortimer asked.

"Anthony Spencer, Figgis and O'Doyle, plus the carriage driver, who could be another one of the Bishopsgate Mob. Then there's Ada and Ingrid and that chap Fuller. Mind you, there could be more. Servants or more members of Figgis's gang."

"Well, I can tell you now that there are two more at least," Ambrose said.

George looked incredulous. "How the devil would you know that?"

"Because, dear George, I was not going to waste my time sitting on that cart. After my little tête-à-tête with Major Hinton-Brown, I found a gap in the hedge and made my way around to the stables. Kept low and took cover in the wood. Ever stalked tigers, George? Best tiger hunter in the Punjab in my day. Stealth's my middle name. Anyway, I set myself up in a little outhouse near the stables and kept an eye on things. Saw that fellow drive the carriage around to the stable yard. Then two men joined him and stood around smoking. One looked like a servant, footman perhaps, a youngish chap. The other was a rough-looking cove, older. One of Figgis's men, I'll be bound. So, that will make nine, at least. Seven men and two women."

George snorted, "Ambrose, you could have ruined the entire enterprise. What if they'd seen you?"

Ambrose bristled, "Damn it, man. Have you not realised by now that I'm not just some old fool? I'm entirely equal to the task of taking on these ruffians and you'd do better to realise that fact."

"Gentlemen. Gentlemen!" Mortimer interjected, "we must have no disharmony among ourselves. Now, let's agree that each of us has something to contribute. With George's two associates and the three of us, we have five. So…"

Verity had watched the clash of male egos with a wry smile. Now she held a hand up to interrupt her brother. "Mortie, one moment. Arithmetic was never your strong suit. We have seven, not five. If you think for one moment that I am going to sit here meekly while you go off on your quest, you have another think coming. I'm sure that Mary will feel a greater sense of reassurance if she sees a female face among her rescuers. And you've discounted Phillip too. Would it not be a courtesy to invite him to join us?"

Mortimer opened his mouth to respond, then thought better of it. He glanced at Phillip, who had risen to his feet. "Mortimer, yesterday you saw me at a low ebb. Thanks to you and Verity, I am much recovered and I would like to play my part. I have a strong personal stake in this business. Anthony Spencer has treated me abominably and, although I took Lizzie for granted, she was my niece. Anthony is behind her death, I'm sure of that, and I owe it to her to make him pay. Please include me in this, Mortimer."

Mortimer looked at George, who shrugged his shoulders, and at Ambrose, who gave him the thumbs-up. "Very well, then. Let's plan accordingly."

At three twenty, their deliberations were interrupted by the arrival of Alfie and Dick Cotton. Mortimer and George went out to meet them in the hall and found to their surprise that they were accompanied by a third man. If a person's character can be read in their face, his features showed a mixture of ruthlessness, cunning and black humour. He had all the physically intimidating features of a Bert Figgis compressed into a body half the size. Though

Mortimer and George towered over him, neither of them would want to meet him in a dark alley.

"Afternoon gents," said Alfie brightly. "Alfie and Dick Cotton at your service and this here is our cousin Benny. Benny the Bastard they call 'im, pardon my French, on account of his parentage and his nature. We thought he'd come in 'andy if there's a bit of argy-bargy.

"Pleased to meet you, gents, I'm sure," Benny said gruffly, extending his hand. Mortimer and George viewed it with some trepidation, expecting a bone-crushing grip, but found his handshake surprisingly gentle.

"Welcome to Thorneycroft," said Mortimer leading the three visitors towards the dining room. "I'm afraid there will be little time for you to rest after your journey. Let us acquaint you with our plans, for tonight we will be putting them into action."

Chapter 28

The evening was clear and crisp, with a waxing gibbous moon lighting their journey to Larkford Grange. Mortimer sat up in the box seat of the barouche, guiding his two bays at a fast clip, with George next to him. Alfie, Dick and Benny sat with Ambrose inside. Following close behind came the dogcart with Verity and Phillip.

Dark clothing was the order of the day.

Before setting out, they'd discussed weapons.

"I have my pistol," George said. "What about you, Mortimer? Do you have a firearm?"

"Can't say I have. Father was not one for weapons of any sort. I have a few stout walking sticks to choose from. That will do for me. There are some pickaxe handles in the potting shed. Your London associates could have them."

George looked at Ambrose. "I suppose you'll be carrying a bejewelled scimitar plundered from some Nawab?"

"Very droll George. Sorry to disappoint you, but I do have a little… surprise, shall we say?" Ambrose replied, arching an eyebrow.

"And you. Phillip? George asked.

"Oh, I'm not much of a one for weapons. Perhaps, if Mortimer might lend me one of his sticks?"

"Certainly," said Mortimer, "let's hope that the use of weapons will not be necessary."

"Have I suddenly become invisible?" Verity said.

"I'm sorry…"

"Or did you think that my tongue would be sharp enough to fell a man?"

Mortimer blinked.

"I will be armed with this," Verity announced, brandishing the object in question.

"A gentleman's umbrella," Mortimer observed.

"To all outward appearances, it is indeed a gentleman's umbrella. However, with a flick of the wrist, it reveals this," she said dramatically, twisting the handle and drawing a short, pointed blade. "A hatpin might not be equal to the task this time, so I discovered this. Ambrose is not the only one who likes to explore the contents of the attic."

At ten-fifteen, they drove at a slow walk past the gates of Larkford Grange. The moon was now obscured by cloud. At the house, George noted lights shining from the ground floor of the east wing. The rest of the building was dark. He looked for the cottage but couldn't make it out in the darkness.

Phillip couldn't contain his obvious relief when Mortimer asked him to look after the horses. The barouche and dogcart could, with some difficulty, be accommodated in the same farm gateway that George and Ambrose had used earlier.

Following the plan that they'd devised at Thorneycroft, the party split into two groups. Ambrose and Alfie set off towards the stables following the route that Ambrose had pioneered that morning. The others walked back along the road to the gates. They stood open. A hundred yards of parkland lay between them and a small copse of trees and shrubs. A stone's throw beyond that, they would find the cottage. George led them in single file towards the copse, giving his full attention to the ground ahead, alert for any unexpected obstacles. Mortimer brought up the rear, keeping an eye out for anyone emerging from the house. Between them, Verity, Dick and Benny trod silently in George's footsteps.

Verity stepped lightly over the grass with her eyes on George's back. The ground was quite firm to begin with, but became marshy as they drew closer to the trees. She hitched up her skirt with her left hand while her right kept a firm grip on the umbrella.

She recalled a heated discussion that they'd had back in the library that afternoon. It still rankled with her. George had just finished outlining his plan for the release of the two captives and their swift passage back to the safety of Thorneycroft. Mortimer had expressed his approval and turned to her, expecting her endorsement. Both men were thrown into confusion when she stood up and uttered a sharp, 'no!'

"What the devil do you mean, no?" Mortimer exclaimed, while George threw up his hands and swore under his breath.

"It's not enough. Yes, of course, we must rescue Mary. Cynthia too. But don't you see that our original purpose was to bring Lizzie's killer or killers to justice?"

"No Verity, damn it. That may be your purpose." George couldn't stop himself from pounding the table with his fist. "Freeing them is fraught with enough difficulty. The last thing we need is to take on a gang of ruthless criminals. Don't you appreciate that our task is made much less difficult now that we know that Mary and Cynthia are held in the cottage rather than the house itself? So we may be able to release them without confronting the Bishopsgate Mob. We release Mary and Cynthia and get the hell out of there. That's all."

"And then, they'll come here to Thorneycroft, with reinforcements, I'll wager. What then?" Verity countered, glaring at George.

"If I could inject a note of sanity into this discussion." Mortimer's voice carried an edge which commanded everyone's attention. "I will not countenance turning this business into a reckless folly. George is right. When we thought that we would have to enter the house, it seemed inescapable that confrontation would ensue. But now, with luck, we can avoid a pitched battle."

"Reckless? For heaven's sake, Mortimer, don't you see?"

"Enough. Stop. Not another word. You forget that it is your impetuousness that has brought us to this. Your insistence on pursuing a dubious theory regarding Lizzie James's death has resulted in the abduction of your friend. The fearful position in which she finds herself is due to your actions every bit as much as those of her kidnappers. And now, you would put us all in jeopardy.

"We will go prepared for a fight, but our aim must be to avoid one. For once in your life, Verity, you will not have your way. I will have your agreement or I will hand the matter over to the police."

His vehemence had shocked her. It was not like him. She'd learnt from childhood that Mortimer disliked confrontation. She'd exploited it and become used to getting her way, not only where Mortimer was concerned, but with people in general. With those of the lower classes, it simply followed the natural order of things, not that she was rude or overbearing, simply confident that her will would prevail. With her peers, she had developed the knack of taking the initiative in any relationship. Being on the front foot, as it were. And it worked. For those higher in the scheme of things, her vivacious charm did the trick.

She'd looked around the room for support. Alfie, Dick and Benny studied their feet. Phillip hurriedly looked away. It was Ambrose's pained expression and slow shaking of the head that did it. With a shrug of resignation, she turned away and resumed her seat.

After a short frosty silence, while everyone gathered their thoughts, it was agreed that their objective lay in freeing the captives, without discovery, if at all possible. If that was not the case, they would use only such force as was necessary to defend themselves and get safely away.

"We have a plan up our sleeves if things turn awkward," George said, winking at Ambrose.

Chapter 29

George pushed his way through the copse, gingerly parting the foliage until he had a clear view of the cottage. Only thirty yards of open ground remained.

There was no sign of life. No chinks of light from the shuttered front windows or around the front door. George retraced his footsteps to join the others. "Take your positions," he whispered.

Leaving Mortimer in the shadow of the copse they approached the cottage. Dick stationed himself at the corner nearest the Grange, on guard for anyone approaching from that direction, while George, Verity and Benny tip-toed to the threshold.

Behind them, Mortimer lit the wick of his shrouded signalling lamp, crouching down and spreading his cloak to shade the light as the flame took hold. With the cover closed, he pointed the lamp at the far corner of the house and the stables beyond, snapping the shutter open and shut twice in quick succession. Counting the seconds, he waited for a response. At the count of twenty, he saw a flash, then another, and retired into the cover of the copse. Ambrose and Alfie were ready if needed.

George stood at the cottage door. Running his hand along it, he skimmed the rough surface until his fingers discovered a keyhole. He motioned to Benny, pointing to the lock. Benny rested his pickaxe handle against the cottage wall and reached into his coat. Producing a short jemmy, he wedged it into the small gap between the door and the frame. Planting his feet apart, he began to take the strain when Verity reached across his shoulder and lifted the latch. The door swung open, creaking on its hinges. "There, George, brains before brawn, I think. Thank you, Benny, we can dispense with the jemmy for now. After you, George."

George winced and crossed the threshold. Verity followed, then Benny, closing the door carefully behind them. George felt in his pocket for his matches and a stub of candle.

They all blinked as the match ignited and flickered as it was applied to the wick. George shook out the match and held the candle aloft.

The room, a parlour of sorts, was almost bare. A floor of rude, worn flagstones. A fireplace filled with cold ashes. Bare walls, stained and cracked. And the only furniture - a deal table with four chairs and a single candlestick as its sole adornment. It had a fresh candle in it, which George lit before handing the candlestick to Verity. All was silent.

Three doors led off the parlour. The door to the left was difficult to open owing to the piles of bric-à-brac and rubbish strewn around inside. That was all it contained. The next door, at the rear of the parlour, revealed a crude, dirty scullery with a stone sink and a cupboard containing a few items of chipped crockery.

Verity turned away and hastened to the third door, throwing it open. She stood in the doorway for a moment, then turned around, shaking her head.

"Nothing, it's bare. They're not here," she whispered urgently.

"Eh? Not here?" George echoed. His mind raced. Had they been moved to the house? Could they already be on their way to be sold into concubinage?

They stared at one another in disbelief.

"My God, George, what are we to do?" Verity's voice was shrill. "Aaagh, what's that?" Her scream reverberated around the parlour's bare walls. She spun around in alarm, almost dropping the candlestick.

"Oh!"

"Begging your pardon, ma'am, I—"

"Benny. You gave me such a start, tugging on my sleeve, what?"

Benny's response was interrupted by the sound of the latch being lifted. George felt in his pocket for his pistol as the cottage door opened, and levelled it at the figure framed there.

"Mr Benson, it's me," Dick hissed. "What's happening? I heard a scream."

Then Mortimer arrived in the doorway. "For heaven's sake, what's happening? There are lights going on at the Grange."

"Give the signal, Mortimer. Now, go," George ordered. "Dick, get back and watch the house. Now, Benny, what the devil was all that about?"

"There, in there," Benny pointed back at the empty room, "there's another door. Must be another room."

Chapter 30

Mortimer sprinted to the copse and picked up the signalling lamp. This time, the shutter opened and closed three times. Staring impatiently toward the stables, he spied three answering flashes.

Ambrose put down his lamp and gave the thumbs-up to Alfie, who ran off past the stables and disappeared into the outbuilding beyond. The fire was set and ready for ignition as soon as Alfie applied a match to it. Straw, wooden boxes, paper, and anything combustible were piled up in readiness, liberally splashed with lamp oil. Alfie watched anxiously as the flame hesitated for a moment, then shot up with a satisfying crackle as it took hold. Leaving the door wide open to allow air to fan the flames, he ran to the stables, releasing the five horses from their stalls, shooing them into the yard and urging them out into the parkland. The smell of smoke in the air stoked the horses' panic as they galloped away, neighing and snorting.

Ambrose and Alfie watched anxiously from the shadows, waiting for a reaction from the house. A muffled cry was their first sign that the fire had been detected. Then lights appeared in the ground-floor windows along the side of the house. A door, twenty feet away from their vantage point, flew open and Ambrose recognised the carriage driver he'd seen that morning. The man ran to the outhouse, which was now well ablaze. Sparks and embers flew around the yard, threatening to spread the fire to the stables and even to the house itself. He turned and screamed, "Fire! Fire in the yard!" Two more men came piling out, looking about uncertainly.

"Tim, get over to the pump!" the carriage driver shouted. "Eddie, don't just stand there, damn you. With me. There are buckets in the stables."

"Right you are, Davy."

Tim stood at the pump in the yard and frantically worked the handle, while Eddie and Davy ran around with buckets, trying to staunch the fire. It was beyond them. The outhouse was engulfed and smoke was starting to billow from the stables.

"Help! We need help here!" Davy bellowed, throwing down his empty bucket and dashing back into the house.

"Our job's done, Alfie," Ambrose whispered. "Let's join the others."

Alfie nodded and led the way around the corner of the house, heading for the spot where Mortimer's lamp had shone.

Ambrose was a footstep away from rounding the corner himself when Alfie's cry of alarm sounded, turning into a choking gargle. He drew back and pressed himself against the wall, his cheek hard against the brickwork.

"Lie still, ya little runt or I'll crush yer skull," said a coarse, Cockney voice. "Let's get a look at yer. Who are yer?"

A groan was the only response.

Ambrose unbuttoned his overcoat and reached inside for the blowpipe he'd found in the attic. The three darts he'd discovered with it, their points protected by pieces of cork, rested in his pocket. He picked one out. Whether its tip retained any trace of poison or sedative, he'd no idea, but he hoped it would prove effective.

He took a quick look around the corner. It told him all he needed to know. The large brute of a man could only be Bert Figgis. The Bishop, Alfie had called him when he'd described the leading gang members to them, back at Thorneycroft that afternoon. Lights were shining all over the house now, illuminating the ground outside. Ambrose studied Figgis's profile, the protruding brow and crooked nose, the virtual absence of a neck and the sheer bulk of the man. He was bareheaded, his bald pate reflecting the light. He poked at Alfie with his stick.

"Speak, ya maggot, who… well, well, now there's a turn-up. I know you, don't I? That weaselly, miserable face. You're one of them Cottons. Albert, no Alfie. That's it. Oh dear, Alfie, looks like your goose is cooked."

Ambrose took aim and blew. The dart struck Bert on the cheek, embedding itself in the jowly flesh. His left hand went to the spot and his eyes flashed in pain and surprise as he plucked it out and threw it to one side. He'd taken a step forward, brandishing his stick, when the second dart hit. It was pure luck, Ambrose conceded later. Bert dropped to his knees and toppled over, bellowing like a wounded bull and clawing at his right eye. Ambrose stepped around him and helped Alfie to his feet. As they hurried away, the sound of Bert's agony faded.

***

George and Verity stood outside the door. It was locked. This one was different. More solid. George tapped it. Thick, heavy timber. He stood back, studying it in the candlelight. The wall was different as well. A brick wall roughly daubed with whitewash.

"It's a cell," he murmured. "They've made a cell. This wall and door are not part of the original cottage. This must be where they're being held." Verity put her ear to the door. "There's no sound, George." She rapped the door with her umbrella, listened again, then shook her head.

George beckoned to Benny. "This won't give way easily. Try it with the jemmy." Benny nodded and examined the door while Verity stood at his shoulder with the candlestick. He struggled to find a purchase between the door and the jamb. The jemmy was too thick. He tried ramming it into the corner between the door and the frame. "It's a tough one, guv," he grunted.

"I'll see if there are some tools," George said. "A hammer, something to force the jemmy in. He shielded his candle stub and crossed the parlour towards the first room they'd looked in. Somewhere among that jumble, he might find something useful. He was halfway across the parlour when he heard the front door latch. Blowing the candle out, he felt for the handle of his pistol.

"George, George," the figure in the doorway hissed.

"I'm here, Dick" George replied, moving towards the door, "what is it, this time?"

"There's merry hell going on over on the far side of the house. Smoke and flames."

"Good. Thanks to Ambrose and Alfie."

"And there's someone coming this way. From the 'ouse."

Chapter 31

Ada Cole hurried outside from the kitchen at the rear of the Grange. Jackie O'Doyle stood at the kitchen door, holding a lantern. "What the hell's happening at the stables?" she asked curtly, fastening her cloak.

"Never you mind about that. Bert and the rest of them will see to it. That young scullery maid, Aggie, said she heard a scream over yonder," Jackie said, nodding in the direction of the cottage. "Could be a fox, she thought. Now then, take this lamp and get across to the cottage and keep an eye on those two. Where's Ingrid, by the way?"

"With Anthony, last time I saw her. Perhaps they've gone to the stables as well."

"All right. You just get along then. I don't know what's going on, but if it's mischief, then someone will wish they hadn't been born. I'll have a wee scout round. Wait for me in the cottage."

Ada set off along the path to the cottage. Jackie watched until she arrived at the front door and disappeared inside.

He worked his way along the side of the house, staying close to the wall; watching and listening but hearing only shouting from the direction of the stables. Reaching the front of the house, he peered out into the blackness of the park. As his eyes adjusted to the dark, he saw the copse, a shade blacker than its surroundings.

A movement, was that? He wasn't sure. A shape? Someone there? Jackie was a creature of the teeming highways, back streets, and alleyways of the East End, but it hadn't always been so. As a lad in Sligo, he'd been raised as a country boy in a dirt-poor family, scratching a living. His father, that drunken old bastard, called himself an agricultural labourer. Petty thief and poacher, more like it. Jackie and his two older brothers were apprenticed to these occupations from an early age. But it was Jackie that excelled at the poaching, developing, along the way, the stealth and field craft that kept him one step ahead of the gamekeepers.

He kept low, blending into the darkness. Step by step, he closed on the copse. He stopped. There it was again. Movement away to his right.

Jackie was handy with his fists and his boots, but so were most of the toughs he came across. It was always advisable to have a little something extra to rely on if things got lively. He patted his jacket, feeling the cut-throat razor in his inside breast pocket, then slid his hand into the outside jacket pocket on the right. You'll do the job, he thought, feeling the familiar weight of the leather cosh in his palm.

Mortimer's left foot had gone numb. Pins and needles from standing still too long. Ambrose and Alfie had replied to his signal. He could see and hear the results of their handiwork in the distance. Now his job was to wait for them to come to him, guiding them with his lamp if necessary. "Bring them to the cottage," George had said.

He stamped his feet to get the circulation going. Where the devil were they? Surely, they should be heading his way by now.

***

Ada lifted the latch and stepped inside, holding her lantern in front of her. Nothing looked out of place. She went to the table and placed the lantern on it, next to the candlestick. That's when it occurred to her. That candle. She'd replaced the old stub just that afternoon. It was new then, but now the wick was black and dribbles of candle wax had run down it and solidified. No - not solidified. They were still soft to the touch and there was that smell of hot wax.

She'd turned on her heel to go back to the door when it struck - a heavy blow to the left side of the jaw which sent her sprawling onto the flagstones. Someone was shining a light in her eyes. She pushed herself up on one elbow, then felt another blow, jolting her head back, and the light went out.

"Not my way, to 'it a woman," Benny grunted, "but that Ada Cole 'ad it coming. That's for my little sister, you bitch," he said, prodding the unconscious form with his boot. Verity wondered what he meant, but thought it better not to ask.

George picked up Ada's lamp and took control. "Here, Benny, gag her with that cravat of yours, would you? Dick, light the candle and go next door and rummage around for something to tie her up with. Rope, if there is some or some rags, we can…"

"No need - look," Dick pulled some lengths of thick twine from his pocket. "Never know when you might need a bit of string," he added with a chuckle.

He and Benny tied Ada's hands behind her back, and bound her feet together. Neither felt any qualms about drawing the twine as tightly as possible, cutting into the flesh of her wrists and ankles.

George stood over the woman, satisfying himself that she was securely tied. "Verity, search her pockets, would you? We need the key to that door."

Verity knelt, feeling in the pockets of Ada's apron. The face just inches from hers was indeed an older, more lived-in version of Ingrid's. The apron yielded nothing. She drew it to one side. The coarse black linen skirt beneath had pockets and there, on the left side, she felt the hard outline of a bunch of keys. As she withdrew them, Ada's eyes opened. They blinked in confusion, then blazed ferociously as she realised her situation. Verity stepped away quickly as Ada struggled against her bonds, voicing muffled outrage beneath the gag.

Benny knelt at her side, pressing down on her shoulders and lowering his head to whisper in her ear. As he spoke, Ada ceased struggling. Her eyes were no longer angry, but large with fear.

***

Jackie crept closer. Just three yards separated them.

Mortimer felt inside his cloak for his hip flask. He took a nip, then another, savouring the warmth of the cognac. Jackie saw him replace the stopper. Now then, he thought, gripping his cosh and taking a step forward.

At that instant, Mortimer moved away to the edge of the copse, raising his arms above his head, waving. Jackie retreated into the cover of the trees as two figures approached across the park.

They greeted Mortimer, and after a whispered conversation, the three of them made their way around the edge of the copse. Jackie emerged ten paces behind and followed at a safe distance until they reached the cottage door. It opened, and they stood illuminated in the doorway for a moment before going inside. He briefly glimpsed someone holding the door open for them. Then it closed.

Jackie's pulse quickened, his breathing, too. He knew the signs; embraced the rage building in him. Jackie, the calculating, cautious stalker, turned into Jackie the vengeful, pitiless nemesis.

Three men. The one he'd stalked and now these two. An old man by the look of him, with a younger chap. What the devil? The tumult over at the stables and now this? But it wasn't the three men that had him shaking with anger. It was her, that figure in the doorway, the one who'd dared to plunge that hatpin into his neck. He rubbed the spot, consumed with one thought only. How much he'd make her suffer.

Chapter 32

They gathered around the locked door. George held the keys. There were five on the key ring. Two were obviously too large for the lock. The third fitted. A half-turn and the lock clicked open.

The stench of foul air came first, then a whimper. He held Ada's lantern up and shone it around the room. Two pairs of eyes reflected the light like wild nocturnal creatures. Verity followed with the candlestick and the pitiful state of the captives was revealed. On two dirty mattresses at the far end of the room, they cowered. Their clothes were ragged and filthy and their hair hung about them in greasy, knotted strands.

Verity handed the candlestick to Dick and rushed forward. "Mary. Dearest Mary. It's me. It's me, Mary. It's Verity." The figure shrunk back, shaking. Verity reached out, gently touching Mary's shoulder and feeling her flinch. "Mary, look at me please," she persisted, taking hold of Mary's hand and stroking it. Mary gave an anguished cry and slumped into her arms, sobbing.

George knelt in front of Cynthia Grant. She stared ahead vacantly, not seeming to notice his presence. "Miss Grant. My name is George Benson. The lady comforting Mary is Verity Mallard. We are here to rescue you. Do you understand? We mean to get you to safety."

Silence. George was about to repeat himself. Then a nod. "Thank God," she said.

Mortimer appeared at Verity's side and helped her to lift Mary, who stood unsteadily, then shuffled to the door with their assistance. Dick helped George to get Cynthia to her feet. She stood for a moment with George holding her arm, then detached herself with a muttered 'thank you,' and walked unaided from the room.

Everyone gathered in the parlour. Ada remained where they'd left her on the floor, with Benny standing guard over her. Mary and Cynthia sat at the table, looking nervously around at their saviours. Verity joined them, smiling encouragingly.

George rapped on the table. "Listen to me, please. Our work is not done. Now, we have, by great good fortune, released Mary and Cynthia from that vile cell, but they and we remain in danger. We must get them away from here as quickly as we can. Fortunately, apart from this creature," he continued, pointing at Ada, "no one at the Grange seems to be aware that we are here. Not yet, that is. Ambrose and Alfie can be thanked for executing their part of the plan perfectly, the stables fire has distracted everyone, but not for much longer. And, thanks to Ambrose, it looks as though Bert Higgis won't be troubling us, but there are plenty of others at the Grange.

"Now then, Ambrose and Alfie, I want you to go back to the carriages. Tell Phillip we have Mary and Cynthia and make sure that we can get away smartly. We won't be far behind. Dick, get back on guard, will you, while Mortimer and I confer for a moment?" The three men nodded and made their way out.

George drew Mortimer aside. "So far, so good. But—"

"George, one moment," Verity interrupted. "They need air - Mary and Cynthia. After that awful fetid room, they must have some fresh air. I'll take them outside. Just outside the door for a moment."

"Oh, well - yes, I suppose. Just for a few moments. Make sure Dick keeps an eye out. We'll join you soon and make for the carriages. Just wait there."

"Come along, Mary, and you too Cynthia, let's get some air." Verity picked up her umbrella and coaxed them onto their feet. Mary turned towards the door. Cynthia made to follow, but stepped aside to look down on Ada. She spat in her tormentor's face, then turned away.

Verity filled her lungs with the clean night air as she stepped outside. The clouds that had obscured the moon earlier had cleared to reveal a star-filled sky. Closing the door behind them, she led them a few paces along the front of the cottage towards the corner where Dick was stationed.

"Dick," she whispered. "Dick, It's Verity."

She'd almost reached the corner when she saw him standing with his back to her. "Dick," she repeated. "Is it...
"

Her voice trailed off. The hat - the bowler. Dick went bareheaded. The realisation hit her, a sickening reminder of that alleyway in Coventry.

"Well, if it ain't the little darlin' as stabbed me with a hatpin," Jackie spun around, flicking his cut-throat open in a slick, well-practised movement. "Oh, and there are those two little apprentice harlots with you, I see."

Verity took a step back. She thought of crying out, but hesitated to risk alerting the other occupants of the Grange.

She pointed her umbrella at Jackie as though to fend him off and took another step back.

"Dear, dear, run out of hatpins, have we? Now that's a right fearsome umbrella you have there," he smirked. "I think I'll just have to take that away from you."

He made a grab for it with his left hand. Verity evaded his lunge and skipped around him. He turned to face her again, not smiling now. He held the razor up, feinted a couple of times, the blade passing inches from Verity's face.

"I've been thinking what I'd do if our paths crossed again," he sneered. "I've thought of slicing through that pretty throat of yours. But maybe I'll just carve your face up a bit. Leave you something to remember me by. Yes, that's what—"

No sooner had Verity seen Cynthia's pale face appear at Jackie's shoulder than the attack was launched. From behind, two hands, fingers curled into talons, clamped themselves on Jackie's cheeks. Cracked nails, black with dirt, gouged and tore at his flesh. One hand scrabbled for his left eye. His reaction was explosive. He broke away, turned and swung his right arm, scything through Cynthia's neck in a welter of blood. She swayed, wide-eyed, for a heartbeat, and crumpled. Verity looked on in horror. Cynthia's blood spread in a dark puddle, reaching the hem of Mary's ragged skirt where she sat quivering, with her back against the cottage wall.

Jackie grunted and felt his face. He'd finish the job now, kill them both, Verity and Mary. Cut their throats. He turned to face Verity again. Laughed, as she attempted to hit him with that ridiculous umbrella. He caught it in his left hand and she let go. He threw it aside. He had her now.

At first, it just felt like a punch. A sharp blow to the abdomen. As if her fists would save her. He gripped the razor tightly, ready to swing. She hadn't moved or tried to run. Another punch, a hopeless, desperate gesture.

He felt the warm wetness soaking into his long johns an instant before the pain. A sharp torment that spread like fire through his guts.

Verity looked at the short, thin blade in her hand. The blade attached to the umbrella handle that she'd released when Jackie closed on her. She backed away.

He stood uncertainly, swaying slightly while the blood soaked into his clothes. The razor fell from his hand. Without a word, he shuffled past Verity, moving jerkily like an automaton. Verity watched as he faded into the night, then wiped the blade on a tussock of grass and picked up her umbrella, sliding the blade in place until the mechanism clicked home.

Mary sat with her head resting on her knees, covering her eyes, quivering. Her sobs were barely audible. Verity knelt at her side.

"Verity, it's time to move," Mortimer called out softly, emerging from the cottage door. "What the devil… George, get out here now."

Mortimer joined Verity at Mary's side while George stepped over to Cynthia's body. A glance was sufficient. "She's dead," he said in answer to Mortimer's unspoken question.

Verity struggled to explain what had happened. She fought to order her thoughts. George and Mortimer waited anxiously as her account unfolded.

"Good God, Verity. When you showed us that umbrella back at Thorneycroft, I never imagined you'd have to use it," said George. "And O'Doyle walked off, you said?"

"Staggered away was more like it. He's badly hurt. The blade went right in. It was that or he'd have slashed my throat as well," she replied, looking over at Cynthia's body.

"Where the hell was Dick? He was supposed to guard the place. Dammit, where—"

"Oh, I don't know. I thought that man was him at first."

"George, behind you." Mortimer pointed over George's shoulder. Dick came around the corner shakily, keeping one hand on the wall to steady himself and rubbing the back of his head. George went over to him. "What happened?"

Dick blinked, struggling to focus. "I… I don't know, Mr Benson. Honest. I just came to and I've got a lump the size of an egg on the back of me 'ead. And… oh my good Gawd, what's happened here?"

"She's dead Dick. Jackie O'Doyle's handiwork. He must have crept up on you. Lucky for you he didn't slit your throat."

Verity left Mary's side. "George, we must get Mary away from here."

"Yes. of course. Poor Cynthia's beyond our help, but I'm loath to leave her lying out here."

"You're not proposing to take her body with us, surely?"

"No, I only thought we might move her to the cottage."

"Very well. Quickly then," Verity urged.

Mortimer and George carried Cynthia into the cottage. Verity and Dick helped Mary to her feet and followed. Benny continued to stand guard over Ada and looked around in alarm at their entrance. "Not now, Benny," George said as he and Mortimer passed through the parlour and into the empty room where they'd discovered the entrance to the cell. They laid her body gently on the floor and stepped back into the parlour.

"Now, let's go," George urged. "We'll make straight for the gate and then to the carriages. Mary, can you walk? It's not too far."

"Yes, if Verity will take my arm, I will find the strength to get away from this awful place."

"And I'll take your other arm," said Mortimer. "We'll soon have you safe in Thorneycroft."

"Outside then, everyone," George commanded.

"What about this one?" Benny asked, pointing at Ada.

"Just leave her. Come on, everyone, outside now."

Chapter 33

"Good evening, ladies and gentlemen, and welcome to Larkford Grange. You might have told me you were planning to visit. Miss Mallard, how nice to see you again. Ah, I see you have become reacquainted with Miss Phillips. I must say she appears to have neglected herself of late. She used to be so well turned out. What can have happened to her, I wonder? Won't you introduce me to your other friends?" Anthony Spencer affected a tone of mock civility quite at odds with the double-barrelled shotgun he levelled at the group as they emerged from the cottage. Next to him stood Davy, the carriage driver, also armed with a shotgun, and Ingrid Lloyd, holding a lantern. In the background, three more men stood watching.

Mary flinched at the sound of her name. Verity put a protective arm around her and held her close.

Mortimer stepped forward, "I am Sir Mortimer Mallard, Verity's brother. You would be well advised to put your weapons aside. We are taking Miss Phillips away with us now. You sir, and your associates are guilty of sickening crimes against this young lady and worse. Your other captive, Cynthia Grant, has been cruelly murdered by one of your henchmen. You'll face the full force of the law, Spencer."

Anthony Spencer held the shotgun steady, pointing directly at Mortimer's chest, wearing an expression of amused contempt until Mortimer mentioned Cynthia Grant. Then it changed.

"Cynthia Grant, nonsense. Don't play games with me. Cynthia Grant is… "

"Dead, with her throat cut by that swine, O'Doyle," George interjected. "There's her blood," he continued, pointing to the dark stain near the cottage wall. "Her body lies inside. My name is George Benson and I'll take great pleasure in seeing you hang." George moved to stand at Mortimer's side, drawing his revolver and aiming it at Anthony.

In the strained silence that ensued, George thought he saw a flicker of uncertainty in Anthony's eyes. An owl hooted away in the distance. Silence again, then a muffled cry.

Anthony and Ingrid looked at one another. "It's Ada," Ingrid shouted, "They've got Ada." She rushed for the cottage door, but Benny grabbed her as she reached the threshold and pinioned her roughly. She screamed her full repertoire of obscenities at him and struggled vainly. "Shoot them, Anthony, shoot the whole damn lot of them. Kill them," she shrieked, thrashing her head from side to side.

George cocked his pistol. "Spencer, there are six of us. Do you really think that you could kill us all and dispose of our bodies as if nothing had happened? Are you really going to pull the trigger yourself? Not your style, surely? You get others to do your dirty work, don't you? And I promise that if I see your finger move on that trigger, I'll put a bullet through your brain before you can pull it."

Spencer took a step forward.

"Now then, man, think. Pull that trigger and it'll be the end of you. Your only chance of evading justice is to disappear. Take off for some bolt-hole abroad and you'd best be quick about it. We'll take Mary to Sir Mortimer's home. It will take an hour or so and then we'll alert the authorities. You have a sporting chance, which is more than you deserve."

Anthony Spencer kept his gun steady, but George noticed his finger was now curled around the trigger guard rather than the trigger itself. Spencer turned his head. "Eddie, run off and get the rest of the men round here right away."

He turned back to George and Mortimer and laughed. "We seem to have something of an impasse, do we not? But when the rest of my associates get here, you'll be hopelessly outnumbered. You can't cover all of us with that little pistol of yours. Perhaps I'll ask the delightful Mister O'Doyle to devise a fitting end for you, and no doubt Ingrid and Ada will be only too glad to assist him."

The two groups stood awkwardly, facing one another. George felt his arm tiring as he tried to hold his pistol steady. Eddie returned in company with five more men. They fanned out in an arc around the cottage. "Ah, good," Anthony announced, "all we need now is… yes, Eddie, what is it? "

"It's Jackie. I'd just rounded this lot up when I found him. He's dead, Mister Spencer. Flat on his back beside the kitchen door. Blood everywhere."

"The deuce he is," Anthony spluttered. "Figgis, did you hear that? Figgis, where are you?" he said, looking around.

"And that's the other thing I was going to say," Eddie continued. "Bert. We can't find Bert. No one's seen him since just after that fire started."

Anthony swore. "Move in, men. Davy, you keep your gun trained on the women. If there's any trouble, give them both barrels."

Benny muttered an oath, throwing Ingrid to the ground and turning to face two of the approaching men. Mortimer moved closer to Verity and Mary, placing his body between them and Davy's shotgun. Dick stood by, hefting a pickaxe handle. Spencer's men closed in.

George shifted his aim to cover Davey. His mind was made up. A few more seconds and it would be too late. He'd shoot Davey first, then Anthony, leaving another three rounds to get away before they were rushed. His finger tightened on the trigger.

Three whistle blasts sounded - loud and shrill. A pause, then three more, and raised voices, some at a distance, others much closer. Anthony's men hesitated. Anthony and Davey looked away, peering into the darkness, their gun barrels no longer trained on George and the others.

"What on earth?" Mortimer muttered as a line of men in civilian clothes carrying firearms materialised out of the darkness. George uncocked his pistol and put it back in his pocket, watching Anthony's men run off towards the house. Anthony hesitated for a moment, then took off after them, Davey hot on his heels. A dozen men ran past in pursuit of them, followed at a more leisurely pace by two men on horseback. The younger of the two followed the pursuers, while the other stopped and addressed himself to Mortimer.

"Sir Mortimer Mallard, I presume. Let me introduce myself. I am Colonel Quilter, late of the Life Guards, but now attached to the Home Office. I see that our arrival came not a moment too soon. You will oblige me by returning to your home immediately. Your carriages are where you left them, and one of my men will accompany you. Tomorrow, I will call on you and take your statements. Shall we say ten a.m.?"

George knew that clipped military voice. That horseman who'd passed him on the road as he went to reconnoitre the Grange.

The Colonel returned his gaze, "aha, we've met before. I see you've cast aside your farm labourer's apparel," he said with a smile.

"Colonel Quilter," Mortimer interjected, "would you kindly tell me what is going on? We are all extremely grateful that you and your men turned up when they did, but…"

"My dear Sir Mortimer, all in good time. Now, it is imperative that these criminals are rounded up. Tomorrow, I will be happy to indulge you, but I must insist that you leave this place at once. Here's my man, Jenkins. He will accompany you."

Mortimer shrugged. "Very well. Mary, are you all right? Take my arm. Lead on Jenkins."

"Just one thing," George turned to the Colonel, pointing at Ingrid, whom Benny had managed to grab before she could run away with the others. "That woman is one of the chief criminals and there's another tied up inside the cottage. And, you will also find the body of Miss Cynthia Grant, she was murdered here in the past hour."

Chapter 34

Verity remembered little of their return to Thorneycroft. She'd wrapped a rug around Mary and held her close as the barouche sped along. Any inclination to discuss the night's events was dampened by the presence of Jenkins. No one spoke. She fell asleep within half a mile.

Colonel Quilter arrived the next morning with military punctuality, accompanied by two younger men. "Good morning, Sir Mortimer. I trust that you and your party are somewhat recovered from your ordeal. May I introduce my two assistants? Mister Ackroyd, whom you saw with me last night, and Mister King, who led another contingent of my men to ensure that the Grange was surrounded."

"So, have you arrested them all? Mortimer asked?"

"I'll be happy to give you a full account of what transpired. But first things first. I would be grateful if you would furnish us with a room where we can take statements from each of you. You obviously stirred up quite a hornets' nest at Larkford Grange. When you've given me a full account of your actions, I'll enlighten you as to why I and my men staged our… intervention."

George and Mortimer, having schooled everyone as to what their statements should and should not contain, Colonel Quilter and his men were treated to a remarkably consistent recital of the events at Larkford Grange.

Alfie, Dick and Benny were permitted to return to London with fulsome words of thanks from Mortimer and a handsome payment for their services.

A sandwich luncheon was laid out in the dining room where the Colonel and his assistants sat around the table with Mortimer, George, Verity, Ambrose and Phillip. Mary rested in her room. Hers had been the last statement taken. With Verity at her side, she'd done her best to answer the Colonel's questions, despite the obvious strain she felt in recounting her abduction and mistreatment.

"Thank you all for your statements," the Colonel began. "If my men and I appear rather drawn and gaunt, it's because we have not slept. Since our timely arrival at Larkford Grange last night, we've been questioning the people we apprehended, several of whom face serious charges and have been handed over to the police."

George stole a quick glance at Verity, receiving an encouraging smile in return.

"Having eliminated those who were genuinely servants," the Colonel continued, "we have identified several members of the Bishopsgate Mob, some of whom have outstanding arrest warrants against their names. However, it is the ringleaders that have commanded most of our attention and, when I say ringleaders, I'm speaking of the principals in a criminal enterprise encompassing crimes of the utmost seriousness both here and abroad.

"Pardon me for speaking plainly, especially with a lady present, but these people are involved in everything from burglary and extortion, to organised prostitution, kidnapping, as you well know, and murder. And we can even add the forgery of works of art to the tally."

He paused to drink from a glass of water.

"Needless to say, Anthony Spencer is the criminal mastermind behind this whole rotten business. Despite his public persona as an apparently successful impresario, his wealth was actually derived from crime. Through his touring companies, he organised thefts from the houses of the well-to-do across the country. This most recent tour of The Importance of Being Earnest coincided with burglaries in most of the towns it visited, Oxford, Cheltenham, and Coventry. Even in Chipping Handley, several items of substantial value were stolen from Mr Sidney Naismith, who had entertained Spencer as a guest."

"I'd wondered about that when Mortimer told me he'd read of it in the newspapers," Verity said. "But are you saying that Anthony carried out these thefts himself?"

The Colonel smiled. "Oh, not he. His modus operandi when planning the tour would involve visiting the various theatres and, being a celebrity, he would often be invited to the homes of prominent local citizens. Thus, he would, in criminal parlance, 'case the joint', that is, identify items of value and assess how vulnerable the premises might be."

"Then use professional burglars?" George asked.

"Precisely, and he had them ready to hand - in the cast."

"How intriguing," Verity said, "which one?"

"Not one, Miss Mallard, but three. Frederick Clarke, Sidney Fuller and Arthur Thomas."

"Goodness, the three old stagers. Who would have thought it? Phillip, would you ever have guessed such a thing?"

"The last people I'd have suspected," Phillip replied. "They seemed so innocuous."

"Well, innocuous or not, it turns out that they have a long history of supplementing their earnings on the stage with burglary," the Colonel said dryly, "and while we're on the subject of cast members, there's the presence of Miss Ingrid Lloyd at Larkford Grange to consider."

"And to think I'd once believed her to be one of the few truly decent cast members," Verity exclaimed. "Yet she turned out to be involved in Mary's abduction through that awful sister of hers, Ada."

"She certainly assisted in planning the abduction, although it was you that they were after, wasn't it?" the Colonel said.

"Yes. I understand that Anthony Spencer had formed the opinion that I knew something that might incriminate him."

"Really? I wonder why?" The Colonel replied. Verity shrugged her shoulders.

Colonel Quilter hesitated as though to pursue the question further, then continued. "However, our Miss Lloyd has more to answer for than that."

"Has she?" Verity and Mortimer said in unison.

"The death of young Miss Elizabeth James at Worcester turns out to have been a case of premeditated murder."

"I knew it!" Verity slapped her hand on the table.

Colonel Quilter raised an eyebrow. "Really, Miss Mallard. How did you come to such a conclusion, may I ask?"

Verity immediately regretted her outburst. If she told the truth, that she knew that Lizzie was engaged in blackmail, she would inevitably be asked to furnish proof. She had no intention of exposing the blackmail victims, particularly as Phillip, with his bigamous secret, was sitting next to her.

"Oh, I simply didn't think that it could be accidental.

Why on earth would Lizzie take it into her head to clamber up onto that gantry? And as for being the worse for drink, well, I never saw her indulge excessively."

The Colonel stared at her for several uncomfortable seconds. "Hmm – your intuition, while clearly not founded on evidence, has proved to be correct. Ingrid Lloyd is to be charged with the murder of Miss James."

"What? How could that be? The monster. How could she? Lizzie had done nothing to Ingrid." Phillip stood up, quivering with agitation.

"She was your niece, I gather."

"Yes, my niece. But why …?"

Verity took Phillip's hand, gently urging him to sit down. "Let's just hear what the Colonel has to say," she whispered.

"Thank you, Miss Mallard," the Colonel resumed, "Mister Aspinall, I realise that this is difficult for you and I shall outline the facts as succinctly as possible. It will at least provide some comfort in knowing that justice will be done. That the police have now charged Ingrid Lloyd is, in truth, a case of good fortune, because of the nervous disposition of Sidney Fuller."

"They arrived at the Grange together," George said. "Two days ago, when I was observing the place."

"Quite so. When we interviewed Miss Lloyd, we were unaware that she had any connection with Anthony Spencer other than as a member of his touring company. She told us she had simply been paying a social visit to Larkford Grange and was innocently caught up in our raid on the property. I must say, it had a plausible ring to it. She clearly has some ability as an actress. It was our later interview with Fuller that brought out the truth. His nerve, or perhaps his conscience, got the better of him. He's turned Queen's evidence, hoping to save his neck."

George emitted a low whistle. "Not just a burglar, then."

"According to Fuller, he'd been unaware that Ingrid was also a criminal associate of Anthony Spencer until she approached him in Worcester. She told him that Elizabeth – Lizzie - had somehow discovered that he and his associates were carrying out burglaries on Spencer's behest and had sought money from Spencer to keep silent on the matter. He insists that Ingrid told him she wanted his help to threaten Lizzie rather than murder her, and that he was duped.

"On the night in question, Ingrid invited Lizzie to stay on at the theatre after the performance, indicating she had information about Anthony Spencer that would be of interest to her. The girl took the bait and as soon as she entered Ingrid Lloyd's dressing room, Ingrid struck her with a hammer, killing her. Fuller was secreted in the room and claims to have looked on in horror. He felt that he then had no choice but to help Ingrid with the charade of forcing some alcohol down Lizzie's throat and carrying her body onto the stage and up onto the gantry. After they'd pushed the body off it, they made it appear as though she'd struck her head on a table."

Verity fought the urge to stand up and shout that she had been right all along, but satisfied herself with nods of acknowledgement from George and Mortimer.

"Has Ingrid confessed?" she asked.

"Not a bit of it. Denies everything. However, she cannot deny her association with Spencer. We now know, of course, that her sister is Ada Cole, and your testimony,

Mr Benson, confirms that she was complicit in Miss Phillips's abduction and subsequent mistreatment at that cottage."

"Yes, that was obvious from the conversation that I overheard."

"Speaking of Ada Cole, our task in apprehending her was most straightforward thanks to your efforts, although one of my men sustained a nasty bite to his wrist when he untied her bonds. She is charged with abduction, of course, as well as several counts of assault against Miss Phillips and the late Miss Grant."

The Colonel paused and picked up a small notebook from the table. He spent some time leafing through it.

"Now, we come to a rather perplexing matter," he said, his searching gaze falling in turn on George, Mortimer and Verity. "According to your various statements, Miss Grant had ventured outside the cottage for a breath of air, together with Miss Phillips. Before any of you could join them, a matter of moments only, Miss Grant had the misfortune to encounter one of the Bishopsgate Mob, Jackie O'Doyle, a violent criminal well-known to the police. Some sort of struggle ensued, and he slashed her throat with a cut-throat razor, killing her. Is that correct?" he asked, directing his question at Mortimer.

"Yes, it happened so quickly. The two ladies went outside. One of our men was stationed there so we thought they would be safe. We only had a brief conversation among ourselves, then we followed. By then, it was too late. All we saw was Miss Grant lying on the ground and a figure running away."

"And could you tell who that figure was?"

"No, it was dark. But Mary - Miss Phillips knew it was

him," Mortimer answered.

The Colonel referred to his notebook again and flicked through a couple of pages, leaving it open in front of him.

"Indeed. Miss Phillips, it appears, did not see the attack take place because, as she put it, 'when Jackie suddenly appeared, I was so terrified, I curled up against the cottage wall and covered my face with my hands. I was paralysed with fear, expecting him to come for me. I must have fainted'. Was it not indeed fortunate that Miss Phillips did not meet the same fate?"

"That might well have happened had we not stepped outside the cottage when we did," Mortimer responded.

"No doubt." The Colonel snapped the notebook shut. "The last any of you saw of O'Doyle was his back as he ran away from the cottage,"

Verity, George, and Mortimer nodded.

"Well, he didn't get far."

"Your men caught up with him?" Verity asked.

The Colonel gave a half smile. "In a manner of speaking. His body was found near the rear of the house. The lower half was covered in his blood. He'd been stabbed twice in the abdomen. So, O'Doyle has escaped justice, although it might be said that a kind of poetic justice has been served. His face had several deep scratches upon it, which we realise must have been inflicted by Miss Grant. We found skin under her fingernails.

"Oh, and we also came across an open cut-throat razor on the ground near the cottage. Strange that he left it there. Perhaps he dropped it accidentally?" the Colonel mused. "So, there we have it. How he met his death remains a mystery. For now," he added pointedly.

"But what about Anthony Spencer?" Verity demanded.

The Colonel considered for a moment. "Of course, Miss Mallard, I will answer that question in a moment, but first let me inform you of another mystery that we discovered last night."

Ambrose fidgeted uneasily in his seat.

"O'Doyle's was not the only body we came across. Outside the west wing, near the stables, we found the recumbent form of one Albert Figgis, alias the Bishop, leader of the Bishopsgate Mob. Stone dead. And, here's the most remarkable thing. He had a dart embedded in his right eye. I'm referring to a poison dart such as certain Amazonian tribes use. I understand that they use a blowpipe. Astonishing.

"So, while you, Sir Mortimer, and your group of rescuers were engaged in and around the cottage in rescuing Miss Phillips, two men met their deaths in mysterious circumstances and a blaze broke out at Larkford Grange stables. Did I not mention the fire earlier? Of course, you must have been aware of the flames and the tumult that ensued."

Mortimer tried to quell the unease he was feeling. "Oh, yes, the fire, a wonderful coincidence. It proved to be a useful distraction," he said hoarsely, his throat suddenly feeling dry.

"Your arrival at the Grange was no coincidence though, was it Colonel?" said Verity. "If you knew so much about Anthony Spencer's criminal enterprise, why had you not moved against him earlier? It seems odd that you should mount your raid at the very same time as our rescue attempt?"

The Colonel exchanged looks with his two assistants, showing a hint of indecision.

"And we're still waiting to hear about Anthony Spencer. You've told us about the others, but not the ringleader," she pressed on.

The Colonel leaned forward. "What I am about to tell you must not leave this room," he pronounced gravely.

"What on earth do you mean?" Verity responded indignantly. "Mortimer, you're a lawyer, tell him."

"Save your breath," said the Colonel curtly, "and I would advise you all to desist from making any statement until you've heard what I'm about to say."

"Spencer is no longer in our keeping," he began, holding up a hand to discourage any reaction. "At this moment, I have reason to believe that he is on his way abroad. His exile will be permanent and he has assumed another identity. I cannot say more on the subject other than to emphasise that it is a matter of national importance that must remain secret. As far as the public is concerned, Spencer escaped and remains at large."

Verity leaped to her feet. "Your raid wasn't intended to bring Anthony Spencer to justice, was it?" she said, struggling to control her anger. "You intervened because you feared that we might capture him ourselves and hand him over to the police."

"This is truly remarkable." Mortimer stood at Verity's side, assuming the inquisitorial tone he'd once employed as a barrister. "A matter of national importance, you say. But what could possibly justify allowing, nay assisting, a dangerous criminal to evade justice? Oh, I know you won't answer, so let me propose a theory. Someone, a very important someone, is implicated in Spencer's wrongdoing." Mortimer glared at the Colonel and pressed on. "What scandal would ensue if that someone's identity were to become known? Could it be a member of the government, I ask myself?" The Colonel stared back impassively. "Or... or a personage of a higher order?"

The merest hint of a tick showed at the side of the Colonel's mouth. He got to his feet. "At the Grange last night, we found the body of Jackie O'Doyle, he'd been stabbed twice with a short, pointed blade. What I didn't tell you earlier was that in daylight, we discovered a trail of blood leading from his body to within a couple of yards of the cottage. So, he was stabbed near the cottage by someone, and the weapon which that person used was not found at the scene. Yet you said that he simply ran off when you emerged from the cottage.

"Albert Figgis was found dead with a poison dart in his eye. How on earth did that happen? And a fire broke out at the stables – hardly a case of spontaneous combustion, I fancy. If I were to summon the police now and ask them to investigate these crimes thoroughly, what might they find? Where might they look for the missing blade and where might they discover a blowpipe? And what if they were to subject those associates of yours from the East End to further questioning – what might they say?

"Consider carefully what I've said, and now I'll bid you a good day", the Colonel said stiffly, motioning his two assistants to follow. He'd reached the door when Ambrose stepped into his path. "So, Major, you turn out to be a colonel, and you were never in Bangalore, were you? "

"No, I deceived you when we met two days ago. I do have a brother in Dorking who once served in the Indian Army. I telegraphed him to enquire whether he had come across an Ambrose Mallard over there. No, he replied, but curiously, he had heard of an Aubrey Mullard. Seems this

Mullard fellow left India under a cloud, something to do with embezzlement, I gather. He's still wanted over there. Coincidence?" The Colonel stepped around Ambrose and walked to the front door. "We'll show ourselves out," he called over his shoulder.

Mortimer turned to George. "What the devil are we to make of that?"

"I'm as perplexed as you are. From the Home Office, he said, and certainly not the police."

"How do we even know that he is who he says he is?" said Verity. "For all we know, this might be some elaborate ruse. He could be an associate of Anthony Spencer."

"Hmm – seems unlikely. After all, he did say that Ingrid, Ada and several others had been handed over to the police. I'll make some discreet enquiries," George offered. "Those two with him, Ackroyd and King, I know their type. They've got the army stamped all over them. NCOs - or at least they were."

"Well, the threat's clear enough," said Mortimer. "We keep quiet about this business or else. You were well out of it last night Phillip, staying with the carriages was the best thing. At least he has nothing to threaten you with."

Phillip smiled weakly and pushed a scrap of paper across the table. "That assistant of his, King, passed it to me. Read it."

Mortimer read the paper and then showed it to George and Verity.

Dare say you will be glad to get back to Mrs Aspinall.
Both of them.

Chapter 35

They let Mary sleep. For two days she only woke for brief periods, to take a little soup before drifting off again. Verity and Mortimer took turns sitting with her during daylight hours and Verity slept on a divan in her room, ready to comfort her when she cried out.

Phillip took his leave, quietly thanking Mortimer and promising to keep all he knew to himself. "I'll take a little while to recover. Then it's back to the stage for me. It's all I know."

George left with him, vowing to keep strictly to the plodding, everyday routine of his private investigation work from now on.

On the third day, Mary declared herself ready to leave her room, expressing a desire for exercise and fresh air. "Could we take a stroll down to the lake after breakfast, do you think?"

"Of course. Shall I ask Mortimer to accompany us?" Verity said brightly.

"I would prefer if it was just the two of us."

They walked as far as the boathouse. Mary said little, responding mechanically when Verity remarked on the mildness of the day or the sight of a pair of swans passing. They stopped at a bench. Verity was content to sit and gaze at the water. She had a strong feeling that Mary was about to unburden herself, but sensed that any encouragement on her part would be counterproductive.

"Verity," Mary's voice was so low that she almost missed it against the sound of a gust of wind furrowing the surface of the lake. "Yes, Mary."

"I'm afraid to shut my eyes, you know. If I shut them, I feel as though I'm back in that awful place."

"Oh, Mary, it broke my heart to see you there. Those vile, inhuman—"

"I said the right thing, you know."

"What do you mean, Mary? What thing?"

"To that man, Colonel… someone."

"Quilter dear."

"Yes, I told him about when he – Jack – Jackie." Mary shuddered. "About when he killed Cynthia and then I said I fainted, saw nothing."

"Yes, Mary. Thank you. Remember, Jackie can't hurt you anymore. He's dead. And those two monsters, Ada and Ingrid, are under arrest. They'll be brought to justice and punished. Severely."

"It happened so quickly. One minute we were walking along that alley. And then – oh God, Verity, I thought they were going to kill me. There were times when I was locked in that cottage when I wished they had killed me."

"Oh, Mary. What can I say? It was me they wanted."

"I know. They kept telling me that you'd soon be joining me. Me and Cynthia."

"Yes, poor Cynthia. Was she any comfort to you?"

"Oh, I don't know about comfort. Not being alone helped, I suppose. If I'd been on my own, I think I'd have died of fright. We talked. She told me things."

"Yes?"

"Anthony Spencer was an acquaintance of her brother. That's how she met him. He encouraged her to become an actress. But there was more to it than that. Her brother wanted her gone, off his hands. Their parents were dead. He just saw her as a liability."

"But Anthony took advantage of her."

"Yes. And he offered her no support when she became pregnant by him. She was desperate and then she lost the baby. When she told him he just shrugged, 'at least you can remain on the stage', was his only comment."

"So, she turned against him."

"She hated him. She said she had two goals in life. The first was to get away from him."

"The second?"

"To make him feel the same despair that she'd felt."

"Go on."

"That's how the blackmail started; she needed money to escape from him. To America, she said. She spied on her fellow actors; started gathering that material. Then she got Lizzie involved, as you know. What will you do with it now, Verity?"

"Why, I'll return it, of course. The photographs, the journal, everything. But there was nothing in that material that specifically compromised Anthony Spencer. Just a vague statement that he was not what he seemed."

"No. It was all in her head. About the forgeries."

"Forgeries? Colonel Quilter mentioned something about art forgery. That Anthony was somehow involved in it. Oh, of course - silly of me not to put two and two together then. Kingsley Grant and he were acquainted you said. My word, why would a painter with Kingsley Grant's reputation stoop to forging works of art?"

"That's exactly what I said to Cynthia," said Mary. "She said Kingsley was given to gambling. He could be quite reckless and was seriously in debt at one time. Anthony came to the rescue, but at a price."

"To produce forged paintings."

"It all started quite innocently, Cynthia said. He had painted one or two small works in the style of the Renaissance old masters. A Raphael was one I think she said. There was no intent to pass them off as the real thing. But Anthony saw an opportunity. He took advantage. Within a year he'd established a business passing off fakes as old masters to buyers in America."

"Did Cynthia threaten to expose them?"

"Her plan was first to get safely away overseas when she'd gathered enough blackmail money. Then she'd inform the authorities here in England."

"So, she didn't plan to blackmail Anthony himself."

"No, she just wanted him to be brought down. And, as she said, he was too dangerous to threaten with blackmail."

"Tell me, Mary. What happened at Chipping Handley?"

"Cynthia received a letter from Kingsley stating that he was leaving to spend some time in the South of France. He told her that when he returned, he expected to find that she had removed her possessions from his London home. That as far as he was concerned, she should support herself and that henceforth he did not wish to have any association with her."

"The cold-blooded beast!" Verity exclaimed.

"Cynthia was incensed. She wrote back and reminded him that she knew all about his forging."

"So, Kingsley told Anthony, and he had her abducted?"

"Precisely. Ingrid invited Cynthia to take tea with her, which Cynthia thought rather strange, but she went. Ada and that awful Bert Figgis were there. Before she knew it, she was trussed up in the back of a cart. They drugged her. Then they held her in a house somewhere in London before bringing her here."

"Tell me, did she talk about Anthony's other criminal exploits, the thefts, the… the prostitution and so on?"

"No. That Colonel asked me the same question. She only talked about the art forgery. It seems she was unaware of the other crimes."

"Well, no matter. The knowledge she had was enough to condemn her. And Lizzie too. There's the irony. She knew nothing about Anthony in reality, but her half-hearted attempts at blackmail must have somehow come to his attention. So, he had her killed just to be on the safe side."

"And the same would have applied to you, Verity. Ingrid was quite blatant about it when she arrived here and came to gloat at us in that cottage. She had searched Lizzie's room looking for blackmail material, thinking that it compromised Anthony."

"But I'd already removed it. So, when I showed my hand, with those alterations to the play, she must have put two and two together. I could have ended up in that cottage with you and Cynthia — and what then? Murdered or sold into a life of degradation?"

Mary grasped Verity's hand. She had a haunted look. "They taunted us," she whispered, "told us things, hateful things about what would happen to us. Istanbul, they said. We would be sold to a bordello there. 'Two or three years of it you can look forward to and when your looks and your health break down, they'll drop you in the Bosphorus'. Oh, my God, Verity, they meant it. I can still see the delight in their faces."

"Mary, please don't be offended but I must ask. Was it just words?"

Mary looked away across the lake, letting go of her friend's hand. Verity watched anxiously, not daring to say more. Mary kept her gaze fixed on the water. Her bottom lip trembled. A tear swelled in her eye and rolled down her cheek.

"They came the night before you rescued me. The three of them." She wiped the tear away. "She knew. Cynthia knew. She tried to fight, kicked out, but they held her down – Ada and Ingrid held her down while he… Jackie," she said, spitting his name out like a foul taste, "he raped her, Verity. I begged them – begged them to stop. I covered my eyes but the sound of it… I wish I could forget that sound."

"Oh, dear God, Mary. Did they …?"

Mary sat stiffly, her hands clasped together in her lap. Verity saw her breast rise and fall as she took a deep breath. A sob came from the back of her throat. "When he – that devil – finished, he came and sat beside me. Put his face up to mine. I could smell liquor on his breath. I wanted to die. Really, Verity, I just wanted to die."

Verity held her breath, fearing to hear any more. Nausea took root in her stomach.

"He laughed at me. 'Well now, that's just a taste of what you can look forward to,' he said, 'not that you'll have handsome devils like me to deal with. Oh no, I can just see you now with some fat old fellow pressing down on you. 'Course, I could give you a proper seeing to just like I did to Cynthia just now, but then you bein' a virgin and all, you'll fetch a much better price. Pity, but there it is.' - I just sat there, listening to Cynthia weeping."

Verity put her arms around her friend and drew her close. Mary went limp and rested her head on her friend's shoulder. The swans drew close to the bank. Verity watched them glide by. In her mind, the blade in her hand plunged again and again into Jackie's guts.

Chapter 36

Montagu Square glowed in the slanting rays of the sun. Verity savoured the gentle warmth of the breeze as she stood at the open drawing-room window. August promised to be a month of languid summer days. Only birdsong disturbed the calm of the evening until a solitary cab caught her attention. She remembered the night, all those months ago, when Mary excitedly announced her professional acting debut as Cecily in The Importance of Being Earnest. She'd been late then and here she was again, twenty minutes after the appointed time.

"Mary's here," she called out as she tripped through the hall and opened the front door. Mortimer emerged from the back parlour with George in his wake, joining Verity on the pavement and taking Mary's hand as she stepped down from the cab.

Mary felt the gaze of three pairs of eyes. Saw the mixture of joy and concern on their faces. She felt awkward, as though she were attending an audition.

The weeks since her rescue from Larkford Grange had seemed like an endless walk along a dark passage. Gradually it would become lighter, but then abruptly the gloom would descend once more. After a few days at Thorneycroft, she'd reluctantly agreed, at Verity's insistence, to enter a private sanatorium. There, her fears and her mistrust of the world were gradually overcome thanks to the care of her doctors and Verity's frequent visits. Bit by bit, she learned to control the terrors that memories of her captivity brought on and to think of the future. Bad days followed the good ones, but less frequently as time passed.

A constant fear in the back of her mind had been the thought of appearing in court as a witness. With Anthony Spencer having disappeared and Jackie O'Doyle and Bert Figgis dead, Ada was the one person charged with Mary's abduction. Mary fervently wished for her to be punished but quailed at the thought of facing her from the witness box.

When she learnt from Verity that Ada Cole had hanged herself while on remand, the surge of sheer relief she felt had been decisive in her recovery.

Mary smiled and returned Verity's embrace, then allowed herself to be swept along into the house.

"My dear Mary," Mortimer announced when they had seated themselves in the drawing room, "it is with the greatest joy and delight that Verity and I welcome you back to this house and to health and happiness after all you have endured." Turning to the table beside him, he drew a champagne bottle from its bucket of ice, filled four glasses and handed them around.

"To Mary," he said, as Verity and George echoed his toast.

Mary smiled and nodded, mouthing a 'thank you', not trusting herself to speak out loud.

"And," Mortimer continued, raising his glass again, "here's to George, without whose steadfastness, good sense and courage, things might have played out very differently. To George."

Toasts over, they sat awkwardly looking at one another, until, in her inimitable way, Verity took matters in hand.

"Who would have thought, Mary, when you announced last November that you were about to become an actress, it would draw us all into a real-life melodrama? I feel like a character in a novel of the racier sort, don't you? In which, after the most awful trials and tribulations, the heroes – and heroines prevail against the darkest of villains. I'm not seeking to make light of it after all that we've been through, but I must confess that when I look back at everything that's happened, it doesn't seem quite real."

"Those novels usually have a neat ending though, don't they?" George remarked. "In novels, the villains are undone, defeated and brought to justice. But that's not the case, is it? Not while Anthony Spencer remains at large. And all to protect someone powerful who, it seems, is above the law. I'm sorry if I put a dampener on what is indeed a joyous occasion, but—"

"Yes, George," Mortimer interrupted quietly but firmly, "you're correct, of course, but nothing we can say or do will alter things. You do appreciate that, don't you? Let's not allow this happy occasion to be soured."

Verity watched anxiously while George sat brooding on Mortimer's words. Abruptly, he looked up and smiled. "You're quite right, Mortimer. Forgive me, Mary, for behaving in such a boorish fashion. It's a great pleasure and relief to see you recovered and in good health. What is it you plan to do now, may I ask?"

"George, really, there's nothing to forgive. I'm sure we all share your disappointment. But," she continued brightly, "I have determined to look to the future and I can tell you all that my acting career is about to resume."

"How marvellous," Verity exclaimed.

"Yes, it is rather marvellous. I haven't told you this before, but I received a visit from Phillip Aspinall just before I left the sanatorium. He was quite his old self. Full of plans to establish his own company. And I'm to become his leading lady."

"Ha, wonderful," said Verity, clapping her hands.

"Yes, indeed," Mortimer agreed.

"We're discussing a new programme. An initial run in London, then off to the provinces."

"Another tour, eh?" said George.

"Well, I did draw the line at returning to Coventry."

"And what of the other members of the company?" Verity enquired.

"Well, there's one that you would know quite well."

"Oh goodness. Not Gertrude, surely," Verity shuddered at the thought.

"Oh good lord no. In fact, I gather that she has retired to live with her sister in Bognor. No, it's Edward."

"Oh, I am glad. He was always a decent soul," Verity responded, adding with a mischievous laugh, "Now that I think of it, you could return those photographs to him."

"Not on your life. I'll arrange for the three of us to meet for tea next week if you like. You can return them then. Now that's enough of me. What about the rest of you? George, still investigating, are you?"

George nodded. "All very dull and worthy cases, I can assure you. Oh, and Alfie and Dick Cotton send their regards to everyone."

"And Benny?" Mortimer asked.

"Benny is currently enjoying a spell at Her Majesty's pleasure. I gather he'll be out by Christmas."

"Mortimer," Mary piped up, "is all well at Thorneycroft? Is Ambrose behaving himself?"

"Ambrose has been a little subdued of late, I must say. His latest passion is bird watching. He's busy building himself a hide down by the lake. Apart from that—"

"Apart from that," Verity jumped in, "Mortimer is engaged to be married. Sorry, Mortimer, I just couldn't hold back. It's to—"

"If you'd kindly allow me to finish, Verity, I'm perfectly capable of telling Mary and George who my fiancé is? I have the honour of being engaged to Miss Olivia Forbes."

"She's the eldest daughter of Professor and Mrs Angus Forbes, Mary," Verity couldn't resist another interruption. "Such a nice girl. Intelligence and beauty in equal measure. Far too good for Mortie, of course."

Mortimer threw up his hands. "I give up. Can't even announce my own engagement without interruption. Now, before Verity can say another word. We are to be married in the spring. We do hope that you will be able to attend, Mary. You too, George."

"Yes, it will be simply wonderful to have us all together for the wedding," Verity said, rising from her seat. "I will have returned from France by then."

"From France? Really?" said Mary.

"I leave in ten days. You know that Mama left me a house in Normandy. I intend to spend some time there. And… it will be such a pleasure to see my daughter again. Now, let's go through to dinner," she added, delighting in the astonishment on Mary and George's faces as she led them out into the hall.

Mary couldn't contain herself. "D - did you say your daughter, Verity?" she stammered, trotting after her friend, with George and Mortimer close behind.

None of them glanced at the evening paper lying folded on the hall table. Had they done so, their attention would have been drawn immediately to an article on the front page. There, under the headline, *Fugitive Impresario – Latest Sighting,* Anthony Spencer's saturnine face stared directly at the reader, the photograph capturing the slick dark hair receding slightly at the forehead, the intense, deep-set black eyes, the clipped moustache and square jaw. The article reported the sighting of a man bearing a close resemblance to Spencer at the Hotel du Palais in Biarritz. This was the latest in a string of claimed sightings since his flight from justice. He had even been reported as far afield as Cairo and New York, but no sighting had been confirmed and this one was no exception. The last paragraph reported that one of Anthony Spencer's partners in crime had been executed that morning. Ingrid Lloyd's death sentence for the murder of Lizzie James took place at 9 am that morning in Holloway Prison.

Acknowledgements

With thanks to Ian Hooper and all at Book Reality for making this book a reality.

About The Author

R J Williams was born in Aberystwyth in Wales and now lives in Perth, Western Australia.

After a busy career in information technology and management consulting, in the UK and Australia, retirement has given him the opportunity to indulge his interest in history and pursue his long-held ambition to become an author of historical novels.

He enjoys writing, cycling, travelling, and volunteering with Para Quad industries, who provide employment to people with disabilities.